W9-BPJ-245

HITMAN

HITMAN

Parnell Hall

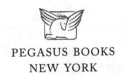

PEGASUS BOOKS
NEW YORK

HITMAN

Pegasus Books LLC
45 Wall Street, Suite 1021
New York, NY 10005

First Pegasus Books edition 2007

Library of Congress Cataloging-in-Publication Data is available.

ISBN: 978-1-933648-53-8

10 9 8 7 8 6 5 4 3 2 1

Interior design by Maria Fernandez

Printed in the United States of America
Distributed by Consortium

For Jim and Franny

1

"I'M A HITMAN."

I sprang from my desk chair, waved my arms. "No, no, no! You didn't say that, I didn't hear that, let's start the conversation again. I'm not an attorney, I'm a private investigator. What you tell me is not a privileged communication. If you confess to a crime, I have to tell the cops."

"I'm not confessing to a crime."

"You just told me you're a hitman."

"That's not a crime. It's a profession."

"I don't care if it's a breakfast cereal. It's a word I don't want uttered in my office. At least not following the phrase, 'I'm a.'"

"*Hit man* is two words. And 'I'm a' isn't a phrase, it's a fragment."

"What are you, a linguist?"

"I'm an English teacher."

"I thought you were a hitman."

"Yeah, but you didn't want to hear that. I teach public school at Harmon High on West Ninety-second."

I sat back in my desk chair, sized up my prospective client. Did Martin Kessler look more like a schoolteacher or a contract killer? It was hard to tell. He was wearing a blue blazer with a white shirt, open at the neck. The jacket was loose, could have concealed a shoulder holster or a pocket of pens. His hair was dark, curly, but not greasy—I chided myself for the stereotype. He couldn't have been more than forty, forty-five.

What had brought him to the Stanley Hastings Detective Agency was hard to imagine. It's a small agency, and I'm it. I have one client, Richard Rosenberg of Rosenberg and Stone, whose TV ads bring in more trip-and-falls than you can shake a private eye at. I am the private eye most often shaken, the old pro, the go-to guy, the longest on the job. Or, as my wife, Alice, puts it, the one without the gumption to get out. (Alice doesn't *really* put it that way, she's actually very supportive; it's just I can tell that's how she feels. A good therapist could get rich off me, if I could afford a good therapist.)

It was the wrong time for such ruminations. I had a hitman in my office. Without admitting the fact, I had to find out why.

"Okay," I said. "You can either leave right now, in which case we have no problem. Or you can tell me what you want, in which case we either have no problem or we have a very big one. Depending on what you say."

"You mean I can't talk about the people I kill?"

I put my teeth together, smiled the fakest smile. "I don't seem to be getting through to you. I not only don't want you to mention such things, I don't want you to allude to such things. I don't want you to tell me you're not talking about such things, I want you to simply *not do it*."

The guy had twinkling eyes for a hitman. I wondered if he really was. "That would make for an awfully tame conversation."

"I can live with that."

"Okay, here's the deal. I've gotten tired of my current occupation, and I'd like to retire."

"What's stopping you?"

"You understand I'm not talking about my position at Harmon High."

"That's for real?"

"What, you think I could live off the other thing? I assure you I can't."

"We're not talking about the other thing."

"I know, I know. We're not talking about anything important. Anything that matters. So, how do you like them Yanks?"

I squinted at him. "Am I being punked? Is some cop laughing himself sick just now?"

"Not about this." Martin Kessler took a breath. "Let me try to explain in terms that don't freak you out. I have two jobs. One is as a schoolteacher. One isn't. I would like to keep my teaching job and quit my part-time one. Are you with me so far?"

"I wouldn't exactly phrase it that way, but I get the picture."

"Here's the problem. My part-time job is not the kind you just up and quit. That is the type of thing that makes an employer unhappy. An unhappy employer is a very bad thing in my part-time job."

"I understand."

"Thank god. Only a moron could fail to, and I'd hate to hire a moron."

"You want to hire me?"

"Oh, god, you *are* a moron. No, I came in here looking for lawn furniture."

"All right. Of course you want to hire me." I frowned. "That's not the way I'd phrase it either. I mean of course that's the reason you're here. *Why* you'd want to hire me I couldn't begin to imagine."

"Aren't you a private eye?"

"In the loosest sense. I chase ambulances for a negligence lawyer. I take pictures of cracks in the sidewalk and help people sue the City of New York."

"Yeah, yeah. I don't really care. Look, here's the deal. I've been given a job. I don't want to do it. But I can't get out of it. It is, and it pains me to say it, an offer I can't refuse. So I can't turn it down. But I got a little time. I don't have to go rushing into it."

"What do you want from me?"

"I want help. I want you to help me *not* do this job. You're not the bad guy. You're the hero, saving the day. Can you live with that?"

I frowned. Against all odds, Martin Kessler had managed to place the concept of working for a hitman in a context that was damn near acceptable.

"What would I have to do?"

"Not much. Follow me around. Watch my back. See if anyone's taking an interest in me."

"Why would they?"

Kessler's smile was pained. "You're unusually slow, aren't you? Of course you compound it by insisting I talk around the subject. Let's just say when a particular name fails to appear on the obituary page, certain people will want to know why."

I shuddered.

"So? Do you want the job, or don't you?"

I had one question. After the tenor of our conversation, I felt more than a little embarrassed to ask it.

"How much does it pay?"

2

RICHARD ROSENBERG HAD A HABIT of ridiculing anything I did. In particular, anything I did outside his private practice. This was generally a ploy to keep me *in* his private practice; still, Richard always seemed to get a kick out of it, almost as if he were sharpening his jaws for court. It didn't matter how sound, sane, or rational a project of mine might be, Richard would manage to poke a hole in it. The full force of his sarcasm and irony could be unleashed at a moment's notice without the slightest provocation.

In this case he had cause.

"A hitman. You're working for a hitman."

"No, I'm working for a schoolteacher."

"Who works as a hitman."

"I said *hypothetically.*"

"*I* said *hypothetically.* Otherwise, *you* wouldn't have said *anything.* You're not getting me involved in your cockamamie schemes."

"What qualifies my scheme as cockamamie?"

"Your hypothetical hitman. Hell, just the fact you have to talk in hypotheticals at all should tell you this is something you shouldn't do."

"I have no choice."

"Why?"

"I've seen his face. If I refused, he'd have to kill me."

It's hard to shock Richard, but that did. His mouth fell open. "Are you serious?"

I wasn't. I was joking. But the moment I said it, it seemed a distinct possibility. Apparently, schizophrenics shouldn't joke about hitmen. A lesson learned too late.

I didn't want to look terrified in front of Richard. I settled back into the depth of his overstuffed client's chair and tried to act nonchalant. "The problem is, this is basically a good guy."

"Who kills people?"

"He has that one personality flaw."

"Which you intend to overlook."

"Which I am not prepared to admit."

"Hypothetically."

"Oh, no, I'm genuinely not prepared to admit it."

Richard smiled, cocked his head. "I'm glad to see the color return to your cheeks. You covered well, but the prospect of your new client rubbing you out clearly took you aback."

"Wait till I tell him you're standing in the way of my working for him."

Richard shrugged. "Nice try, but I doubt if he'd go for such convoluted logic. That was what you were implying, right? That he would rub me out to obtain your services. I'm sorry, but that's too stupid to be scary."

"Yeah, look, I gotta give this guy an answer."

"When?"

"Tomorrow morning."

"He can wait that long?"

"It's a casual hit. Not pressing. As a pro, he makes his own schedule."

"So how will they know he's not doing it?"

"That's what *I* said. Apparently, there's a reasonable period of time in which there is an expectation of success."

"I'm sure that's how he phrased it."

"Actually, the guy's an English teacher."

"I don't want to know."

"Right. Anyway, is there any reason why I shouldn't do this job?"

"Aside from sanity, logic, and a moral sense of right and wrong?"

"Yeah. Aside from that."

Richard steepled his fingers. "You *have* a job. You work for me. You may not count that as an obligation, but, trust me, it is. I depend on you."

"You have other operatives."

"Operatives? Did you really just say *operatives*?"

"You have other investigators."

"They're not nearly as good."

"Then I should make more money."

The suggestion was my usual conversation stopper, but Richard steamed right through it. "You know you have to be in court."

"What?"

"You're testifying in the Fairbourne case. Or have you forgotten?"

"Of course I haven't forgotten." I certainly had. I never testify in court, and when I do, it's no big deal, usually about serving papers on the defendant. "Can't you get a continuance?"

"Oh, sure. I'll shoot right over to the hospital and tell the quadriplegic with the spinal cord injury who needs money for the experimental surgery that could let him breathe on his own that I'm terribly sorry, I hope he won't mind waiting, but my witness has to help out a hitman."

"Boy, talk about loading an argument."

"You loaded it. I just pulled the trigger."

"That doesn't even make any sense, Richard."

"Maybe not, but it sounded good. The point is, you lose. No way you can justify this one."

"Right," I said. "I'll just tell the widow with the two little children that I'm really sorry I couldn't keep her husband alive but I had to be in court helping a negligence lawyer rip off an insurance company."

Richard smiled. "You'd have made a good lawyer."

"I'm not ruthless enough."

"Too bad. So tell the guy you have to be in court."

"When?"

Richard consulted his Daily Planner. "Friday."

"This Friday?"

"No. Next week."

"Next week? No problem."

"Oh? You'll be done by then? What makes you think so?"

"Well, it stands to reason."

"It doesn't stand to reason. If the hit *were* going down, you'd be done by then. No problem, piece of cake, the guy's dead, it's over. But if the guy's *not* going to do the job, it's open-ended. It'll never be done unless you fail. At which point either the mark will be dead, the shooter will be dead, or you will be dead. Or some combination of the three. Any of which will terminate your employment. Is that a fair assessment of the situation?"

"Fair to whom?"

"So tell the guy you got a previous engagement, you're willing to take the job, but you're busy next Friday."

"He may not like that."

"I know how he feels. Anyway, this job is apt to result in the death of someone before then. In the event you aren't the one deceased, you would be free to testify."

"And if it isn't . . . ?"

Richard smiled his patented thin-lipped smile. It was what

poker players would call a *tell,* heralding the arrival of the most calmly delivered, devastatingly scathing sarcasm. "In the unlikely event the matter is not resolved, don't you think that a person who kills people for a living could manage to stay alive for a few hours without relying on a private eye whose, dare I say, *expertise* is more in the field of photography than self-defense?"

It occurred to me, long about then, that I wasn't getting anywhere with Richard Rosenberg.

I decided to try Sergeant MacAullif.

After all, how bad could it be?

3

"YOU FUCKING IDIOT!"

I hadn't expected MacAullif to be pleased. And he did not disappoint. A burly homicide cop who'd shared in some of my adventures, Sergeant MacAullif was always torn between helping me out and shoving me through a wall. Today he seemed to be leaning toward the latter.

"Well, what would you like me to have done?"

"Did the phrase 'No, I don't kill people' ever occur to you?"

"That's a clause."

"What?"

"It has a subject and a predicate."

"What the fuck are you talking about?"

"Nothing. I've just been brushing up on my English grammar lately."

"Well, bully for you. Would the motherfucking, cocksucking, sequence of words 'No, I don't kill people' have any significance to you other than its grammatical classification?"

10

"I'm not going to kill anyone."

"Or associate with those who do."

"*You* associate with those who do."

"I *arrest* those who do. I don't accept employment from them."

"Bullshit, MacAullif. What about undercover cops? Don't they get hired by dope-dealing psychokillers all the time?"

MacAullif exhaled through clenched teeth, emitting a high-pitched whistle. Dogs in Coney Island perked their heads up. "Why are you here?"

"I told you. I have a hypothetical problem. I thought it would interest you."

"Well, think again. I'm a little busy this morning, what with *actual* homicides, not hypothetical ones that haven't even happened yet."

"You're saying I shouldn't have brought you this?"

"If wishes were horses."

"Hey, I'm the good guy here, keeping John Q. Public alive."

"No, you're the bad guy. In my office with something I don't wanna hear. Asking for help I don't wanna give."

"I didn't ask for help."

"Then why are you here?"

"Well, actually . . ."

"Oh, shit."

"You have any mob connections?"

"I've seen *The Godfather.*"

"That isn't what I meant."

"What do you mean?"

"It's a little tricky."

"You're lucky I don't run you in. That's probably what I should do. Arrest you, put you in the box, and sweat it out of you."

"Sweat what out of me? I'm willing to tell you the whole thing."

"I don't want to know the whole thing."

"You're not making any sense. What *do* you want?"

"You could get out of my office. You could pretend you never

came. You could go about your business and I could go about mine."

"It wouldn't bother you that you ignored this lead?"

"A hypothetical? Of course not."

"Okay."

I got up, headed for the door.

"Hey! Where you going?"

"I'm getting out of your office, like you said."

"Come back here!"

I went back and sat down.

MacAullif glowered at me.

"So," I said. "What do you want to know?"

"Never mind the hypothetical bullshit. Why are you here? What do you want?"

"I assume you're not going to assign a cop to help me."

"That would be a good guess."

"You have resources I don't have. In terms of checking people out."

"So?"

"If I were to give you a name, you'd be able to run it down, see if the guy was connected, and, if so, to whom."

"To whom? You really are watching your grammar."

"You'd be able to tell me whether this was a person I should be dealing with."

"I can tell you right now, this is a person you shouldn't be dealing with under any circumstances."

"You don't know the name I'm going to give you."

"You mean it isn't him?"

"I'm not saying it is. I'm not saying it isn't. Just someone I want you to check out. There's no reason why you shouldn't. It might be totally unrelated to what we've been discussing."

"And what have we been discussing?"

"Nothing. We've been talking hypothetically."

MacAullif opened his desk drawer, took out a cigar, and drummed it on the desk, a habit he had when I was pissing him off. He drummed cigars on his desk a lot. "Why do you want me to trace this name?"

"Do you want to know?"

"Of course I do."

"Guy wants to marry my daughter. I want to see if he's a good risk."

"You haven't got a daughter."

"Damn. It sounded so plausible."

"What's the name?"

"Martin Kessler."

"That's the guy we've been talking about?"

"Obviously not."

"Why do you say that?"

"Because I haven't got a daughter."

"Go on. Get the hell out of my office."

"You'll trace the name?"

"I'm not saying that."

"What are you saying?"

"I'll like you better when you're gone."

I got the hell out of his office.

4

"WHY DOES HE WANT YOU?"

Alice put her finger right on it. Which was not surprising. My wife has a knack of zeroing in on the heart of any issue. Or at least she appears to. When Alice is on a roll, I can barely get a word in edgewise. Not that it would do me any good. Alice can argue that black is white or up is down so convincingly that I haven't a prayer of contradicting her. Indeed, she is the master of the Socratic method, leading me though a series of questions that come to the inevitable conclusion. Hers. She is so good at this that the only way I know to deal with her is to attempt to figure out what her position is and then adopt it, leaving her nothing to push against. This is fine in theory, but even in such situations Alice can prove me wrong.

"He wants me because—"

"No, he doesn't," Alice declared, and I knew I was in trouble.

Alice was at the computer multitasking, and she had so many screens open I had no idea what she was up to. Not that I cared. I was somewhat distracted by the fact Alice was dressed in a T-shirt and panties. Our son, Tommie, has gone off to college, and we are empty-nesting. To Alice, it means dressing casually. To me, it means something else entirely, though Alice dressing casually certainly has something to do with it. And tends to cloud my judgment.

Anyway, I hadn't a prayer. Under any circumstances, Alice is a formidable opponent. In a T-shirt and panties she is invincible.

"You don't even know what I was going to say," I protested.

"It doesn't matter. You're wrong. That's not why he wants you."

"Okay, why does he?"

"I have no idea."

"Then how do you know I'm wrong?"

"How do I know anything? Stanley, there's not a reason under the sun that you can come up with for why this guy wants to hire you that could be anywhere close to the truth."

"I dispute that."

"Be my guest."

"Excuse me?"

"Go ahead. Make your case. Why do you think you're right?"

"Alice—"

"I can't wait to hear this."

"I didn't say I thought I was right."

"You think you're wrong?"

"I didn't say that either."

"Well, you're not advancing a very forceful opinion. Can you see why I'd have trouble believing it?"

"Alice, I have no idea why he wants to hire me. I can think of several reasons why he might."

"Big deal. So can I."

"For instance?"

"He doesn't know you're a wimp and thinks you can help him."

"I'm surprised you married a man of whom you had so low an opinion."

"I didn't marry a macho jerk. I married an actor. If I'd known you were going to become a private eye, I might have reconsidered."

"You're arguing on both sides of the issue."

"No, I'm not."

"You're faulting me for not being macho and saying you'd hate me if I were."

"What's your point?"

I had no idea. All I knew was I was stuck in an argument from which there was no way out with the possible exception of walking the dog. Unfortunately, Zelda was curled up on the couch sound asleep. I'd have to poke her to walk her.

"What do you want me to do?" I asked. This was a good tactic, courteous, compliant, eager to do the other's will. Alice hates it, since its purpose is to force her to venture an opinion. Alice's opinions are as elusive as they are strong. I would have more luck pinning a greased pig. The pig, at least, couldn't talk its way out of it.

"It's not what *I* want you to do," Alice countered. "It's a question of what's right."

"You want me to do what's right?"

"Did I say that? I don't recall saying that. What I want you to do might conflict with what's right. And where would we be then?"

"Where?"

"What I want you to do is what you want. Because if you don't do what you want, you'll wind up frustrated and unhappy, and I'll have to deal with it."

Uh-oh.

"So, what do you want?"

You notice how neatly the whole thing turned back on me? Just when I thought I might get out from under. Actually, I knew better. When Alice sets me in her sights, there is no escape.

"I don't want to cause anyone's death."

"That's an admirable sentiment."

"Alice—"

"Sorry. Go on."

"The only reason I'm even considering it is the prospect of saving someone's life."

"Ah. My hero."

"The guy wants out. You think I should set up roadblocks in his path?"

"You're not causing anyone's death. Goodness sakes, Stanley. You think you're the only person in the world who could keep this guy from carrying out his task?"

"Is that a new T-shirt?"

"You go out to buy shoes. The first store doesn't have any that fit. Do you give up buying shoes? No. You go to another store."

"It's hardly the same thing."

"Why not?"

"The clerk in the store can't bust you by giving the cops your shoe size."

Alice spun away from the computer. "You think he'd kill you?"

"No."

"You thinking of turning him in?"

"No.

"You seem more sure about that."

"I *can't* turn him in. I don't *know* anything. The guy claims he's a hitman. He could be a nut. He could be a cold-blooded killer. I have no way of knowing. But if I tell the cops he's a hitman, he's not going to like it. And since the cops will have absolutely no reason to hold him, they'll have to let him go, and he'll be one pissed-off hitman."

Alice spun back to the computer, clicked on an icon, typed something in, shrank the screen again.

"What was that?"

"An instant message."

"What?"

"I'm on AOL Messenger. I just typed an instant message to Mindy."

"Please tell me it had nothing to do with what we're talking about."

"Just a little."

"What?"

"I told her you're being adorable."

"Alice!"

"I didn't say you were being adorable about a hitman."

"So, what are you going to tell her I was being adorable about?"

"The computer. You're always being adorable about the computer."

"Since when is *adorable* a synonym for *incompetent*?"

"See?" Alice said. "I can quote you on that and she'll be none the wiser."

I sighed. "Great. Okay, I gotta go."

"Where?"

"I'm meeting him."

"The hitman?"

"Don't call him that."

"I don't know his name."

"It's Martin."

"What's his last name?"

"If I told you, I'd have to kill you."

"That's very funny."

"Yeah," I said. "Adorable."

5

Martin Kessler was meeting me in my neighborhood, which seemed rather considerate for a hitman. But I understood why he didn't want me in his.

I met him at Carne, a steakhouse on the corner of Broadway and 105th. Alice and I order out from there a lot. They make great burgers, and they have a chopped salad with steak that Alice likes. The restaurant has an elevated bar overlooking the dining area. Not that it mattered. Still it seemed the sort of thing you'd want in a movie setting.

I sat at the bar, ordered a Diet Coke.

"Will you be having dinner?" the bartender asked.

Carne served people at the bar. A man and a woman were already eating. Another had just ordered.

"Not sure yet."

My answer seemed to satisfy him. He gave me a Diet Coke, started to run a tab.

I sat back, looked around. It was early, but the place was filling up. Carne was still doing well, even with Henry's across the street, and the popular new French restaurant, Café du Soleil, in the middle of the block. The neighborhood was really getting classy. Soon Alice and I wouldn't be able to afford it.

At the end of the bar was a TV, tuned to a sports channel. It was too early for the Yankee or Mets game, but a young NASCAR driver was telling a reporter why he hadn't gotten killed in some horrific crash they kept showing over and over. To me, the miracle wasn't why he hadn't gotten killed, but why he was still driving.

Martin Kessler came in. I saw him in the mirror behind the bar. Tonight he looked more like a hitman than a frumpy English professor, but perhaps I was just projecting. He wore a gray pinstripe suit and striped tie. Well, so what? Surely there were men in pinstripe suits and striped ties who had never killed a soul.

In the movies he would have slid onto a barstool next to mine, but the ones on either side were occupied. Worse, there was a vacancy at the other end of the bar. Inconvenient, since he'd told me not to recognize him. I wondered how he planned to handle that.

Martin Kessler bellied up to the bar right next to me, snapped his fingers at the bartender, pointed to the TV, said, "Do you get rugby?"

Bartenders field questions of all kinds; still, that probably wasn't among the top ten. In light of which, he handled it pretty well. "Not right now, we don't. TV's on ESPN till seven, when we switch over to the Yankee game."

Kessler nodded. "Fair enough. Can I get a Dewar's on the rocks?"

The bartender went to make the drink.

Kessler jerked his thumb at the TV. "You like this NASCAR shit?"

"I will if they get it on Staten Island. Be a lot of accident claims to investigate."

"You an ambulance chaser?"

"Yes, I am." I lowered my voice. "How long do we have to keep this up?"

"Not at all. I just thought it would give you a thrill."

"I don't want a thrill."

"You want the job?"

"I don't know if I want the job."

"You were supposed to think it over."

"I thought it over."

"You talk to anyone about it?"

I hesitated.

He shook his head. "That's bad. Very bad. You want to stay in this business, you either come in with a denial right away or not at all."

"I don't want to stay in this business."

"Nor do I." He chucked. "Sorry. I should have said *neither*. *Nor* just sounded more literary. Like a British spy, maybe. Which is what you seem to equate this with. Never mind. Are you going to help me?"

"Tell me why I should."

"Oh, dear. You want a moral justification. Besides saving someone's life. I can't understand why that argument's not persuasive. I suppose it's because you can't see the fellow. Put a name or a face to him. So he's just a statistic. Like a soldier killed in the war. Two thousand. Three thousand. The death toll builds up. More every day. You can't get excited about just one."

"That's not it."

"Sure it is."

"No, it's not. You told me yourself. You're not going to kill this guy."

"Could you keep your voice a little lower?"

"It's a plot for a movie. We're discussing a plot for a movie. People do it every day."

"I'm happy for them. Nonetheless . . ."

"All right, all right," I conceded, lowering my voice. "The point is, you're not going to do it. All you want me to do is keep my eyes open, see if anyone's noticing you're not."

"You know that because that's what I told you."

"So?"

"I lied."

"What?"

"That's not what I want you to do."

"Good. Because I wouldn't be any good at it."

"Yet you were considering taking the job."

"Yeah. I'm a bad person. I don't know how you can bear to deal with me."

"Touché."

"Well, if it's not asking too much, what *do* you want me to do?"

"What you said before."

"Excuse me?"

"The job I have to do."

"What about it?"

"I want you to stop me from doing it."

"Who's the guy?"

He shook his head, signaled the bartender for another scotch.

"Come on. Who's the guy?"

"I can't tell you that."

"How am I going to protect him."

"You're not supposed to protect him. You're supposed to stop me."

"Isn't that the same thing?"

"Not at all. You could protect him by arming him to the teeth, placing him in police custody, or sending him to Tahiti. None of which would involve me at all."

"They'd stop you."

"Not directly. They'd merely remove the need for me to be stopped."

"So how am I supposed to stop you? You want me to shoot you?"

"I'd rather you didn't."

"Then how?"

"By your magnetic personality. Your winning ways. Your powers of persuasion."

I shuddered. "The guy's as good as dead."

"Probably. Look, if you follow my trail, there will come a time when I either carry out my mission or not. At that point you can make a substantial contribution."

"How?"

"It will be obvious. For instance, if you see me about to off some poor dude, you can say, 'Hey, you don't really wanna do that.'"

"Can you be serious?"

"I am being serious."

"Suppose I did that. What would happen then?"

"I'd either take your advice or ignore it."

"What if you ignore it?"

"Then you've done the best you could."

"And I'd get paid?"

"Is that your real concern?"

"It's a big one. I'd hate to get scared out of my wits for nothing."

"Not to mention the moral dilemma."

"So, who's the guy?"

"You don't need to know."

"I'll know if you make a move on him."

"If you figure it out yourself, fine. By then it won't make any difference. Beforehand it would be a disaster. You're compassionate. Considerate. Kind." He reeled them off as if they were dirty words. "You'd want to warn the guy. Help him. It would be a real mess. On the other hand, those qualities are why I want you. You'll bust your tail tying to stop me. What could be better?"

"I can't think of a thing," I said dryly.

"So, will you do it?"

"I'll let you know."

"When?"

"Tomorrow."

He grinned. "Checking me out, eh? Good. You're careful. I like that. Okay, I'll call you tomorrow. You let me know."

"You're leaving?"

"No. *You're* leaving. I'm sitting here having a drink. On your stool. Like that's what I was waiting for. Like I don't know you at all."

I got up. "Good."

"Yeah," he said, sliding onto my barstool. "I thought you'd like that."

6

MacAullif was in a good mood. Of course, all things are relative, and I've grown accustomed to him chewing a bucket of nails while he talks, biting the heads off and spitting the points in my general direction. But a thoroughly at ease and perfectly pleased MacAullif was not what I was used to dealing with. It was like he had a DANGER signal flashing a warning behind his head.

I decided to walk right into it. "You traced that name?"

MacAullif smiled and nodded. It was one of those nods where he just kept nodding. And smiling. And nodding.

"You being a cop and all, I assume you had no trouble."

"None at all. Perfectly straightforward."

"You got everything there is to get?"

"That I did."

"You mind sharing the information?"

"Ordinarily, I would weigh my answer. I would stop, consider what you have a right to know and what you don't have a right to know."

"Well, that's to be expected."

"Yes, it is. Only, in this case, I don't feel the need to do so."

"How come?"

MacAullif picked up a file folder from his desk. "Let's see. Martin Kessler, English teacher. Harmon High. Thirty-six years of age. Married. Two children. And here's the shocking part. Criminal record."

"He has one?"

"That he does. About three years ago, he made an illegal left-hand turn at West End Avenue and Seventy-second Street. Cops pulled him over, nailed his ass. And it's not just the ticket." MacAullif waggled his finger. "That's a moving violation. That's points on your license. That goes on your driving record. I tell you, this is one bad dude."

"That's it?"

"What do want, a written confession? The guy got nailed, paid his fine, cops put him back on the street. Probably hated to, but they couldn't hold him, what with him pleading guilty and paying the fine."

"You're telling me this is a model citizen? What about ties to the mob?"

"What about 'em? Unless he has a bumper sticker, I BREAK FOR MAFIA MEMBERS, the guy is clean."

"You're sure of your sources?"

"As sure as I need to be."

"What's that supposed to mean?"

MacAullif's eyes twinkled. "Yeah, right. You and your hypothetical. 'I'll give you a name. Maybe it is, maybe it isn't.' I don't know how you pulled that name out of your ass, but he's not the guy. Anytime you get good and ready to give me the *real* name you want traced, just say the word."

"That *is* the name I want traced."

"Yeah, right."

"Damn it, MacAullif. If the guy's in deep cover, don't you expect he'd check out clean?"

"Not this clean. This is squeaky clean. This is the-PTA-never-got-pissed-off-at-him clean. This is no-coed-ever-accused-him -of-scoping-out-her-tits-during-class clean. This is no-female-teacher-ever-complained-about-him-making-lewd-jokes-in-the -faculty-lounge clean."

"There's a charge for that?"

"Yeah. Bein' a horny prick and havin' a dick. These days, if someone doesn't accuse you of sexual harassment, you're either shy or gay."

"You ever think of running for elective office, MacAullif?"

"No. Why?"

"Probably just as well."

"Anyway, you couldn't come up with a guy this good. You must have had this name in your hip pocket just waiting for a chance to use it."

MacAullif leaned back in his desk chair. His grin was mocking. "Anytime you want to give me the name of your real hitman, feel free."

7

ALICE WAS TOTALLY SUPPORTIVE. Under the circumstances, overly supportive. She was also braless, wearing a scoop-neck T-shirt that transported me back to my adolescence every time she leaned forward.

I'd swung by home after MacAullif, not to play no-peekie with Alice, but because I had no cases, having cleared my workload to be free to handle the hitman.

Which I'd agreed to do. In light of MacAullif's findings, there was no reason not to. When Kessler called my cell phone, I told him I'd start that afternoon.

Then I went home and told Alice.

Alice, predictably, was unpredictably less upset about me taking the job than she was about MacAullif. "He's being a jerk," she asserted.

"He's not being a jerk."

"Sure he is. Ridiculing you like that."

"He thinks I'm putting him on."

"He doesn't think that."

"He said he did."

"Yeah, but he has to say something."

"He acted like he thought that."

"How did he act?"

"Like he was having a good time."

"See? He's worried. If he was really having fun with you, you wouldn't know it. He'd be putting you on and laughing up his sleeve."

"I think you're wrong."

Alice went on as if she hadn't heard that assessment of her opinion. "See how he's being a jerk? He's taking a bad situation and presenting it to you so that there's nothing further you can do."

"He offered to trace another name for me."

"You got another name for him to trace?"

"Of course not. He's the guy."

"Of course he is. MacAullif's being a jerk."

"He traced him and got nothing."

"That should tell him the guy's a pro. He'd have to be to have a spotless record."

"He had a moving violation."

"I bet MacAullif got some mileage out of that."

"He seemed to enjoy it."

"I bet he did. The prick."

"Alice—"

"Stanley, did you stop to think *why* MacAullif is having so much fun?"

"Because I made an utter fool of myself."

"Talk about ego."

"What?"

"You'd see a lot more clearly if you didn't define everything in terms of you."

"Alice—"

"I'm *not* you, so it's easier to take you out of the equation. What is MacAullif doing? He's sweating bullets. He's been presented with a situation that might blow up in his face. What if this guy that he checked out actually killed someone? That's gonna be embarrassing as all hell. Does MacAullif want to face that possibility? He most certainly does not. He ridicules the theory. But it's scaring the shit out of him."

"I think you're overreacting."

"*I'm* overreacting? How did you feel when he told you the guy was clean?"

"I thought we were keeping me out of it."

"Oh, no. We were keeping you out of MacAullif's evaluation. Never mind. The main thing is MacAullif checked the guy out, came up empty. Which is good. He's paying cash. Still, you wouldn't want to be working for a deadbeat."

"That's the least of my problems."

"You think so? Take a look at the monthly bills."

She had a point. Living in Manhattan isn't cheap. Even with rent stabilization we were barely getting by.

"I can work for Richard."

Alice blinked. "What?"

"I don't have to pick the guy up until this afternoon. I can do some cases first."

"I thought he was paying you by the day."

"So?"

"He's paid you for the day. You gonna work for someone else?"

"Absolutely. I'm gonna work for Richard. I'll call the switchboard, tell 'em I'm on the clock till three."

"You gonna tell the guy you're doing it?"

"No. Why?"

"You don't think he has the right to know?"

"I don't think he gives a damn, as long as I do what he wants."

"You really took the job?"

"It seemed the only thing to do."

"Yeah, sure."

"Well, what would you think of me if I said, 'Screw it, go ahead and kill the guy'?"

"Oh, you idiot," Alice said.

She leaned forward to pat my head, and I forgot what we were talking about.

8

"I'LL HAVE TO HEAR IT from Richard," Wendy/Janet said.

Richard Rosenberg's two switchboard girls had identical voices. I never knew which one I was talking to. Not that it mattered. Neither had the brains of a turnip.

"Okay," I said. "Put him on the phone."

Wendy/Janet gasped. She always did when I talked like that. The prospect of bossing Richard around was more than she could handle.

Richard came on moments later. "You're back to work. So, the job's done?"

"No, but the hours are flexible."

"I don't like the sound of that."

"Why not?"

"Flexible things stretch and bend. I don't like the idea of my cases getting short shrift."

"Richard, your cases are trip-and-falls. I could do 'em in my sleep. I'm going stir-crazy sitting around. I need the work."

"You just sitting around?"

"Yeah. Why?"

"You talk to MacAullif?"

"Why do you ask?"

"So you did. You realize that'll hang you, if things don't work out."

"What could possibly go wrong?"

"Yeah. All right, you want work, I got work. Hang on."

I heard the buzz of the intercom, Richard's voice saying, "Pick up line one," then a click and Wendy/Janet's voice saying, "Yes?"

"Stanley's on the clock, give him work," Richard said, and hung up.

Wendy/Janet paid me back for going over her head to Richard by giving me the worst case she could find. Maybe I'm just projecting. Still, the crack house in East New York in which one Yolanda Smith lived had to be way up on my list of least desirable abodes. The two black guys on the front steps had about three front teeth between 'em, and that was counting top and bottom, and one on the side. The tatters they were wearing were fine for the summer. In winter their balls would have frozen to the stoop. Neither had shaved in this millennium, nor ever seen a comb. Somehow or other, these unprepossessing souls had managed to score enough drugs to get high. Either that or their brains were just permanently addled. But they looked at me without fear or loathing or even the slightest interest as I marched up the rickety steps and pushed open the front door. Neither rain, nor snow, nor strung-out homeless junkies . . .

On the first-floor landing a slightly more upscale clientele were smoking crack. You could tell they were more upscale because they *had* crack, not to mention a crack pipe and a butane lighter. They probably took me for a cop, because no white man in a suit and tie who wasn't a cop would ever be there. They made no move to hide the drugs. If I was gonna bust them, I was gonna bust them. Not much they could do about it.

The guys on the third floor were mainlining crystal meth. I

wondered if that was a step up from the crack smokers, or a step down. I'm just not up on drug etiquette. Anyway, they were sharing needles and probably HIV. I tried not to appear terrified as I gave them a wide berth.

On the next floor I found Yolanda.

Her story blew me away.

The problem with the negligence business is you build up a contempt for your clients. No matter what your good intentions, the job quickly wears you down. Part of it's the monotony, and the repetition, and the fact that each case seems exactly like the one before. But it's also the fact that your clients aren't the most intelligent people in the world. Not that intelligent people wouldn't call Richard Rosenberg, but, in point of fact, intelligent people *wouldn't* call Richard Rosenberg. They'd go to their own or some friend's recommended lawyer, not some guy they saw on TV. So, for the most part, we're talking about people who tend to fall into the category of greedy, indolent, and not particularly bright. Sort of hard to root for. Sort of hard to work up any enthusiasm for their cases. Add to this the fact that the people most likely injured themselves through some stupid action of their own, and it's really hard to care.

Yolanda Smith was something else.

For one thing, she was gorgeous. A light-brown-skinned African-American woman, lithe, large-breasted, though not disproportionately so, twenty-three years old, mother of two.

For a few fleeting moments, a mother of three.

Usually, I ask questions and take notes.

Yolanda, I just listened to.

A welfare mother with two kids living in a crack house in East New York gets her big break, meets Mr. Right, a young whiz-kid, hip-hop record producer who's gonna to put her in rap videos, gonna make her a star. Meanwhile, she's gotta earn her keep.

I sighed.

"Not like *that*." Brown eyes flashing. "He no pimp. He le*git*. He *real.*"

"Go on."

"He gotta friend. Inna business. Movie business. Not porn. Jus' playactin'. No sex. No danger. Like HIV. Unnerstand?"

"The sex was simulated?"

"Ain' no sex. Jus' skin. Give me 'nuff to live on, with the welfare check."

"So what happened," I prompted.

"I *tellin'* you what happen. All parta what happen. Is *why* it happen." She took a breath, composed herself. "Director, he say the rap work inna bag. Only I gotta wait 'cause he can' use no big bitch inna video."

"Big bitch?"

She looked at me as if her estimation of my intelligence, never high, had just dropped a few notches. "Like *big*." She patted her tummy. "Don' work for a song."

"He can't use you in a rap video if you're pregnant?"

"Tha's right. Is on hold, he say, till the kid. After that, he line me up wit' someone like Snoop Dogg, only he ain't got him."

"And what went wrong?" I said, gently urging her toward the point.

"I tell you what went wrong. You don' listen, you don' hear."

In a less attractive woman, it would have been rude. In her it was spunky.

"I'm listening. Go on."

"I's inna hospital. An' the baby come. Only it ain't right. Lotta pressure. Lotta pain. Doctor say, 'Shit!'"

"The obstetrician?"

"Head's not down! Tha's what he say. Head's not *down*!"

"It's a breech?"

"Tha's right. Is a breech. Baby can't breathe. Baby gotta come out now!"

35

"The baby was in fetal distress. The doctor had to do a C-section."

"Right. He gonna cut me. Sean say no."

"Sean? Who's Sean?"

"Director."

"The director. He was there?"

"Yeah."

"How come? Is he the baby's father?"

"Could be."

"And he said no?"

"Tha's right. He say don' cut her. Baby come natural."

"And the doctor listened?"

"Sean, he persuasive."

"I don't understand."

"He don' want me cut. For the video. For my career."

"If you had a C-section you couldn't be in rap videos?"

"Not with a *scar*. Not *there*."

"Did he order the doctor as the boy's father?"

"No. He jus' tell him."

"Is his name on the birth certificate?"

"What birth certificate? Baby *dead*."

"Did you write him down as the baby's father? When you checked into the hospital?"

"No."

"If he wasn't the father, what was he doing there?"

"Lookin' out for his investment."

"And he told the doctor not to do a C-section, and the baby died?"

"Tha's right."

"What was the cause of death?"

"Couldn't breathe."

"Asphyxia?"

"Yeah."

"Because the doctor tried to do a vaginal delivery?"

"Tha's right."

"Did you tell the doctor not to do it?"

" 'Course I did."

"What did you say?"

"Said save my baby."

"And he didn't?"

"No."

"I still don't understand. How come the doctor did what Sean said?"

"They buddies."

"Huh?"

"He and the doc. Tha's why Sean had me go to him."

Jesus Christ.

Like I say, most of the cases I get are simple and straightforward. Some idiot falls down because he is too dumb to look where he is going. He then sues anyone he can think of for his broken leg.

Occasionally I get a case that is so egregious, so clear-cut, so black and white, and so despicable in its nature, that it makes me want to turn the system upside down if necessary, to right a wrong, to see an injustice is avenged. They don't come often, but, when they do, god, how they shake me up.

The bad thing about my job is most of the time you don't care. The worst thing is sometimes you do.

9

MARTIN KESSLER DIDN'T WANT ME to pick him up at school. That doesn't sound right. That sounds like I'm carpooling. What I mean is, he didn't want me to stake out his school and start tailing him when he got out of class. Which I quite understood. Teachers with tails don't get tenure. Sounds like a PI novel. He didn't need me following him then anyway. I didn't know why, and I didn't really want to know. Probably the guy we were supposed to whack didn't get off work that early.

Anyway, Kessler didn't want me going anywhere near his school, so he met me at my office. That also gives the wrong impression. It's not like he came upstairs or anything. At four fifteen, he was waiting for me outside. I came down, spotted him staking out the place. As instructed, I gave no sign, just turned and headed west. He followed me on the other side of the street. At Broadway, we changed positions without ever appearing to do so. I turned south, toward Forty-second Street. So did he, but since he'd been on the downtown side of Forty-seventh Street and I'd been on the uptown side, I was now behind him. I tagged along for two blocks, then crossed Broadway, and paralleled his actions from the other side of the street.

Kessler had told me this was only a trial run, so I shouldn't be nervous. That made me nervous. I felt like I was auditioning. Which would have been fine, since I didn't really want to get the part. Only I was concerned about how he might inform an actor who wasn't hired.

Kessler caught the light at Forty-third Street and crossed Broadway, which changed our positions again. I slowed to let him catch up and pass me but otherwise paid no attention. Not following anyone. Just a businessman on his way home.

We were heading for Times Square, which did not cheer me. If you ever want to lose someone, that's the place to do it. The Forty-second Street subway station used to be somewhat confusing, but they've remodeled it. Now it's totally confusing. Which is only to be expected, considering half the trains in the Northern Hemisphere meet there. If Kessler wanted to test my mettle, that was the place to go.

But when I hit Forty-second Street and turned right toward the newly renovated subway entrance, guess who wasn't there?

Good guess. Instead of going down in the subway, Kessler had walked past the entrance and was admiring the *Lion King* marquee across the street.

Okay, two can play that game.

I walked by the subway entrance, walked by Kessler, continued on down Forty-second Street toward Eighth Avenue.

Hoped like hell he was tagging along behind.

He was. I ascertained that when I stooped and tied my shoe. The oldest trick in the book, but damned if it doesn't work. From down on one knee you can see in all directions without being too conspicuous. It's a nice position, assuming someone doesn't kick you in the ass or steal your wallet.

Anyway, Kessler was tooling along, just your average out-of-town, sightseeing hick without a care in the world.

Excellent. If I stayed on my knees a bit longer, he'd go right by me. But he was gawking at the Wax Museum like he'd never seen it before, and there's a limit to how long one can tie one's shoes.

I got up, continued on down the street.

Forty-second Street's changed a lot in the last twenty years. There are two movie theaters on the corner of Eighth Avenue, but they don't show porn; they're huge multiplexes, showing legitimate flicks. The AMC has twenty-five screens. The Loews, with thirteen, probably has screen envy and gets spam about being embarrassed in the locker room.

The movie seemed as good a ruse as any. I popped in the front door of the Loews, pretended to be checking out the films.

Kessler didn't go by. I know because I was looking out the glass door for that to happen, and when it didn't, I started to freak out. If I was doing this poorly on the doesn't-matter, bullshit, dry-run part of the assignment, I hated to think how I'd do when it was the real deal.

While I was having a meltdown, Kessler came in the door and stood looking at the movie times on the illuminated sign over the box office.

Good god, was the guy actually going to the movies? If so, I hoped it was one I wanted to see. With my luck, it would be some god-awful chick flick. Surely a hitman wouldn't go to one of those, would he?

I headed for the street. It was either that or see a movie, and I didn't feel like one. If Kessler bought a ticket, I could change my mind. I would be too far away to see which one he bought. But it didn't matter. The theater was far from full, any ticket would get me in, and I could follow him to any show.

Having worked all that out, I was almost disappointed when he came out the front door. As usual, he didn't look in my direction, just turned and sauntered by. He walked to the corner of Eighth Avenue, stopped at the light.

Okay, was he going to go west across Eighth Avenue or south across Forty-second Street?

Tough call. The light was green on Forty-second Street and traffic was going through. But the WALK sign was flashing DON'T WALK, indicating the light was about to change. A man who didn't want to sprint across the street could wait for the lights to recycle. Assuming he was heading west. Or he could simply be waiting for the light to change, if he was heading south. He wasn't doing anything helpful, like facing any particular crosswalk. No, he was just hanging out on the corner, looking around, as if he didn't know where to go.

That made two of us.

I was coming up on the corner. I had to make a move or I'd wind up standing right next to the guy. Which he wasn't going to like. And I'd hate to piss off a hitman.

The light changed, and traffic streamed up Eighth Avenue. Well, I was looking for a sign from god. How about one that said WALK?

I joined the flow of pedestrians crossing Forty-second Street. If Kessler followed me, good. If he waited for the light to change and crossed Eighth, I'd cross Eighth, too, and follow him from the south side of Forty-second. If he went north up Eighth Avenue, he was a total asshole, and if I lost him, it was his own damn fault.

Not to worry. A casual glance backward when I hit the sidewalk showed that Kessler was right on my tail. Which should mean he was headed down Eighth. I tested the theory, walked two doors south, and stopped to check out the window display.

There was a Mickey Mouse watch for $14.95. Surely that couldn't be an original Mickey Mouse watch. Then, again, what was a fake Mickey Mouse watch? How would you tell? The hands have five fingers? Could you get busted for selling knock-off

Mickey Mouse watches? Who had the patent? Walt Disney. Who's dead. His estate, but—

In the store window I caught the reflection of Martin Kessler walking by. He was going south on Eighth. For what purpose, I had no idea, but mine not to reason why. The thought that the quote ended "Theirs but to do and die" did not cheer me.

I fell in behind, wondered how long we could keep up our tag-team tailing act.

We kept it up until Thirty-fourth Street, when we reached Penn Station. Was that our destination? It seemed unlikely, since it takes up the whole block. Seventh Avenue and Thirty-fourth Street would have been Penn Station, too. If we were going there, why had we crossed to Eighth?

I was speculating on a lot of things that didn't really matter. It occurred to me the reason I was speculating on a lot of things that didn't really matter was I was pissed off on the one hand and scared shitless on the other. A veritable crazy quilt of excremental functions.

Where the hell were we going?

Kessler stopped at the southeast corner of Thirty-fourth and Eighth. In front of us was a taxi stand with a row of cabs waiting to pick up passengers coming from the trains. Diagonally to the left was the entrance to Penn Station and an escalator down to Amtrak. Would he go in there? If he did, no problem. But I can't go in unless he does and I don't know if he's going to. Why the hell is he so damn indecisive? Jesus Christ, it's like tailing Hamlet.

I walked a little ways down Thirty-fourth Street. I was heading back toward Seventh Avenue, which made no sense, but nothing I was doing made any sense. At least I could see which way Kessler went. If he chose the door to Penn Station, I could wheel around and follow. Likewise, if he continued down Eighth. Basically, it was a good vantage point from which to double back.

I didn't have to. Kessler came tooling right by me.

I wanted to shoot him. Poor choice of words. But here we

were, heading toward Seventh Avenue for no discernable reason. If this was an audition, it wasn't fair. The job wouldn't be as hard as this. The job would be following a *sane* person with a sense of purpose. True, that purpose might be the elimination of a human being, but—

I stopped.

I gawked.

Uh-oh.

I realized why I was having such a hard time following Martin Kessler.

He was following someone else.

10

I FOLLOWED THEM TO AN apartment building on East Eighty-ninth Street. I use the term *followed them* loosely, as in detective fiction. It cannot possibly describe the circuitous, hopscotch, follow-the-leader, duck-duck-goose entertainment I was treated to. It included a trip to my office, by the way, where I pretended to go back to work, but emerged from the lobby the second the coast was clear, just in time to hop on Kessler's trail. I had a feeling I wasn't supposed to. The fact Kessler had taken me back to the office was a pretty good indication the day was over, a rather strong hint that my services were no longer needed, that he wanted me to leave him alone.

Tough luck, buddy. Hitman or no hitman, you've made contact with your quarry. This is the very thing I hired on for. No matter what you want. You made that crystal clear. I'm here to thwart your wishes. My day ends when I say it ends. All right, buster, you think you ditched me, what you gonna do now?

Kessler hopped in a cab, went straight to an apartment on East

Eighty-ninth Street. A modern high-rise with a liveried doorman at the front desk. I watched from across the street while Kessler went in and spoke to the doorman. I could see the doorman shake his head, but Kessler wasn't taking no for an answer. He was still arguing with the doorman when a taxi pulled up, and the guy he'd been following got out.

Kessler greeted him warmly. Even from across the street I could see the smile on his face.

But not the guy. The guy wasn't smiling at all. And who could blame him? If he had the slightest idea he was in trouble. And surely he must, or he wouldn't have *been* in trouble. The guy had to know the arrival of Kessler wasn't good news. Still, he shook Kessler's proffered hand.

Moments later the two men were walking toward the elevator.

Holy shit.

Moment of decision. Is this where I rush in and yell, "No! Woodsman, spare that tree! Hitman, put up your gun!"

Fat chance. There was no way to do it. I'd never get by the front desk.

The elevator doors closed. I could see the lights of the numbers of the floors begin to change, though I couldn't make them out at that distance.

Before I had time to think about it, I was crossing the street, striding into the lobby.

The elevator stopped at 16 just as I hit the front desk and realized I didn't know what to say. Panicked, I resorted to the truth. Or the half truth. Actually, a complete fabrication, but who's keeping score.

"The tenant who just came in," I said, pointing to the elevator. "Was that Freddy Foster? I was supposed to meet him here."

The doorman was all smiles. "Freddy Foster? There's no Freddy Foster here."

"He looked just like him. Are you sure?"

"Sure, I'm sure. That's Victor Marsden."

"New tenant?"

"Lived here for years." He frowned. "Sure you don't mean the other guy?"

Yes, I do. Thank you for the prompt, oh helper-out of us of little intellect and slowness on our feet. "Yes, of course. The guy *with* the tenant. Freddy Foster. Gotta be. You don't know him?"

"Afraid not."

My mind was going a mile a minute, below the national average but top speed for me. "Could you call up and ask the tenant, what's his name?"

"Victor Marsden."

"Yeah. Ask Mr. Marsden if that's Freddy Foster with him."

"Who shall I say is calling?"

This was a moment of truth. I wanted to say Stanley Hastings. That would rock Martin Kessler in his sockets, if Victor what's-his-name relayed the message. But I didn't want to leave my right name, on the alarmingly real chance this apartment building became a crime scene. That would not be a good tidbit of information for the doorman to pass on to the police.

"Rollo Tomassi."

"Huh?"

"Rollo Tomassi," I repeated. A name from the movie *L.A. Confidential* based on the James Ellroy book. A made-up name Kevin Spacey uses to identify his killer. If Martin Kessler knew the reference, it would have to shake him up.

The doorman rang through. "Mr. Marsden? I have a Mr. Tomassi here—"

"*Rollo* Tomassi," I corrected.

"I have a Rollo Tomassi here. He wonders if the gentleman with you is Freddy Foster. He thought he looked like him." The doorman listened, said, "Freddy Foster." Then, "No, *his* name is Rollo Tomassi."

The doorman hung up the phone, shook his head. "You got the wrong man."

I smiled. "Sorry. I could have sworn."

I went out, crossed the street, walked west. I kept going till I was out of sight of the doorman, assuming the guy hadn't followed me into the street. I ducked in the doorway of a brownstone, looked back. There was no one in sight. Why should there be? I hadn't done anything suspicious, anything that would tip off the doorman. Unless he knew the scene from *L.A. Confidential.* I weighed the odds of that. Wondered if doing so made me a bigot.

Martin Kessler came out the front door and looked around.

I ducked behind a car before he could see me. Or so I thought. He walked up, flushed me from my hiding place.

"What the hell do you think you're doing?" he demanded.

"What you hired me for."

"What do you mean, what I hired you for? I hired you for a specific purpose."

"Yeah. To keep the mark alive. That's what I'm doing."

"That was you who called upstairs?"

"Yeah. You like that?"

"No, I don't like that. What a bonehead play. If the guy wasn't suspicious before, he is now."

"Does he know who Rollo Tomassi is?"

"I don't know and I don't care. I took you back to the office. Couldn't you leave it at that?"

"No, I can't. You wanna get rid of me, fire me. Otherwise, I'm gonna do what I was hired to do."

"Fine. You've done it. Now go home."

"But—"

"Are you a total moron? The doorman saw me. With the guy. Going up in the elevator together. Do you think that right now in this apartment would be the ideal time and place to bump him off? I ditched you for a reason. So you wouldn't get yourself in trouble.

You're meddling in things you shouldn't. When you don't need to. When there's no reason. Are we clear?"

His face looked pretty hard for an English teacher. It occurred to me if I were in his class I sure wouldn't wanna be late with a book report. "Yeah. That's clear."

"Good. I'm going to get into a taxi. If you follow me, I'll kill you."

He stepped out in the street and hailed a cab. It went to the corner, turned down Second Avenue.

Another taxi came by and I got in.

I didn't say, "Follow that cab!"

I let it take me home.

11

ALICE WAS SHOCKED. "You saw him."

"Yes."

"You know who he's going to kill."

"Yeah, but he didn't kill him."

"Not yet."

"He says he doesn't want to kill him."

"If he doesn't want to kill him, why is he following him?"

"It's his job."

"It's his job to kill him."

I frowned. "Yeah. But—"

"But what?"

"It's my job to stop him."

"And you did that?"

"Not really."

"I didn't think so. You didn't do anything, did you?"

"No, I didn't. But in a way I did."

"How do you mean?"

"I think just being there is enough. Just the fact that I'm there, a witness, seeing what's going on, is enough of a deterrent to keep him from doing it. So, as long as I'm following him, I can prevent him from doing the job."

"That's one way." Alice added chopped garlic to whatever she was cooking on the stove. It was some lamb dish or other, and I'm sure she didn't know the name of it. Alice doesn't cook from recipes. She makes what she calls a mishmash, inventing as she goes. It's always delicious.

Alice was cooking late tonight because she didn't know when I'd be home. Usually, when that happens, we order out. I think tonight she was cooking because she was nervous and wanted something to do.

"What do you mean, that's one way?"

"There's another way."

"What?"

"Go to the police."

"I've been to the police."

Alice set the wooden spoon on the edge of the saucepan, turned to face me. "Oh, come on, Stanley. What do you mean, you've been to the police? You fed MacAullif a bullshit story, got MacAullif to trace a name. At the time you had no hard information. Now you do. You know who the guy's going to kill."

"I don't know for sure."

"Oh, come on. Is it the guy or isn't it?"

"It's the guy."

"Do you know his name?"

"Yes."

"What is it?"

I hesitated.

"Right," Alice said. "If you told me, you'd have to kill me."

"Actually, if I told you, *he'd* have to kill *me*."

"That isn't funny, Stanley. It's way beyond funny. These are people you should not be mixed up with. If there's any way out, you should take it."

"For instance?"

"I said *if*. I didn't say I knew one."

"I'm open to suggestions."

"I told you. Go to the police."

"And tell 'em what? That the English teacher they've already checked out now has a specific target in mind?"

"Tell MacAullif the whole thing from beginning to end. Leave nothing out. And for god's sakes, don't say *hypothetical*."

"What?"

"The minute you say *hypothetical*, he thinks it's all bullshit. You gotta level with him. This is what happened, this is what I did, I may have broken a few statutes along the way; if so, I gotta take my lumps, but I'm trapped, I can't get out, and I don't want anyone to be killed."

"You want me to turn myself in?"

"I'm not saying turn yourself in. I'm saying get yourself off the hook."

"By turning myself in."

"Well, if you wanna argue semantics."

"Semantics."

Alice dropped pasta into boiling water, added a little salt. The tiniest of distractions, yet it totally threw me. Not that I wasn't thrown already.

"What do you know now that you didn't know before?" Alice said.

"What do you mean, before?"

"Before you took the job."

"I know the mark's name and address."

"That is a fairly important piece of information."

"I also know the hitter's not going to pop him there."

51

"Hitter?"

"Yeah. It's better than *hitman*. Nonsexist."

"Stanley. I'm not in the mood."

"What about wine and candlelight?"

Alice groaned. "You're impossible."

"I'm not impossible. I'm joking bravely in the face of death. I'm not happy with the current situation, and I would love to get out of it any way I could. Short of making a full confession and doing time. The point is, the guy's safe for tonight. The shooter's not going to take him out in his apartment."

"Shooter?"

"You didn't like *hitter*."

"I don't like *shooter*."

"How about *shitter*? Combination of the two."

"Stanley."

"So he's safe tonight. And he's safe tomorrow morning, too, because our hitman has school."

"If he's for real."

"So I have until class lets out at three forty-five."

"To go to the police?"

"Actually, I'm doing cases for Richard."

"Until three forty-five? When you pick up the hitman at school?"

"No, he picks me up at the office."

"What?"

"He doesn't want me going near the school. So he's coming by the office instead."

"What if he doesn't show?"

I sighed, said nothing.

"Stanley."

"I know, I know. I gotta go to the cops."

"You'll talk to MacAullif?"

"I'll talk to MacAullif."

"Before three forty-five?"

"Yeah."

"What about your cases?"

"I'll fit it in between my cases."

"You won't let Richard talk you out of it?"

"I'm not even dealing with Richard. I get beeped by Wendy/Janet."

"Okay. When you talk to MacAullif, remember one thing."

"What's that?"

"Don't use a hypothetical."

12

"Suppose I gave you another name."

"Have you got another name?" MacAullif said.

"Suppose I did."

"This is a hypothetical?"

"No. This is a let's-suppose."

"What's the difference?"

"Semantics."

"You're really pissing me off."

"You should talk to my wife."

"What?"

"I'm a walk in the park. Get my wife in here and see how long you last."

"What's your hypothetical this time?"

"My hypothetical is a let's-suppose."

"This is the name of the hitman?"

"Not necessarily."

"What does that mean?"

"I'm not sayin' it is, and I'm not sayin' it isn't. But it just might be a major player in this little drama."

"Major player?"

"One of the two main participants."

"Are you talking about the whacker or the whackee?"

"That sounds like self-abuse."

"Good. If the hitman offs himself, it's a suicide, and I don't have to find a perp."

"That isn't what I meant."

"I know what you meant. I just can't believe you've regressed to adolescent masturbation jokes."

"I got a name, MacAullif. And I *really* need it traced before three this afternoon."

"Why?"

I took a breath. "I'm in trouble. I need help. I think I'm in over my head. By three o'clock this afternoon I need to know if there's any reason under the sun why anyone would be interested in Victor Marsden of East Eighty-ninth Street."

"He's the victim?"

"Not yet."

"Say I do this for you. You gonna tell me what's up?"

"When I can."

"When's that?"

"I don't know. Alice says I should tell you now. Only problem is, I don't wanna go to jail. And you probably don't either."

"Good guess."

"Would you like me to tell you everything—including the part that could be considered quasilegal—in order to better allow you to extricate me from the unfortunate situation in which I now find myself?"

"You do and I'll kill you."

"Not you, too."

"Your life has been threatened?"

"Only in jest. I hope."

"If your life has been threatened, it's something else. Do you have any reason to believe that this person means to do you harm?"

I took a breath. It would be so easy just to say, "Yes. I'm scared to death. The guy's a wacko whacker who's having far too much fun with this assignment. Who might easily knock me off just to test his reflexes."

Only that wasn't the case. Martin Kessler posed no threat to me as long as I didn't cross him. Which was all well and good, except my *job* was to cross him.

"You're sweating," MacAullif said.

"It's hot."

"I'm a sergeant. My office is air-conditioned." MacAullif cocked his head. "Has this guy threatened your life? Is that why you're sweating?"

"I wish it were that simple."

"It is that simple. There's the good guys and the bad guys. You line up on one side or the other. At the end of the day you tally the score. If you align yourself with the bad guys, don't expect to score very high."

"Where did that analogy come from?"

"Damned if I know. Some guy puttin' together some task force or other, trying to hearten the troops. It's a bunch of bullshit, but what do you expect from a dumb cop."

I noticed how adroitly MacAullif had led the conversation away from the topic of my telling all. I wondered if Alice would appreciate the significance of the timely digression. Except I knew she wouldn't. She'd say, "Bullshit. He pulled that on you because you weren't straight with him." The fact he didn't *want* me to be straight with him would get lost in the shuffle.

"Can you run the name?"

"Of course I can run the name. I have nothing else to do. I sit here all day long, waiting, *hoping* you will show up in my office and give me some work. The five open homicides—make that six—the six open homicides I am supervising can pretty much take care of themselves, seeing as how we have made no arrests and have no one to interrogate. Oh, wait a minute, that's *not* a good thing, is it? Since the commissioner tends to view arrests as progress. And lack of them as—wait a minute, I've almost got it—lack of progress. Which tends to make the commissioner grumpy.

"But now all that is solved. I can tell the commissioner the reason we haven't arrested anyone is because I was busy running security checks on schoolteachers for a private eye."

Luckily, I got out of there before MacAullif spontaneously combusted from an overdose of irony.

13

RICHARD ROSENBERG WASN'T HAPPY. "I hear you're still working for your client."

"Who told you that?"

"Wendy or Janet. I'm not sure which. Says you can't work a full day and you're turning down cases."

I'd turned down one case to go see MacAullif. I'd kept in most of them. The one in New Jersey was out of the way. I'd never have fit it in.

"I didn't have time to go to Jersey."

"You had time to go to Brooklyn."

"I was in Queens. They're neighbors, you know."

"So what are you doing here when you could be in Jersey?"

"I had a case I did yesterday. I wanted to tell you about it."

"What case you did yesterday?"

"Woman with the dead child."

"Oh, that. I'm kicking the case."

"What? A medical malpractice resulting in death?"

"Be a tough one to prove."

"You're kidding."

"It's a high-risk medical procedure. Things go wrong."

"This is more than a medical malpractice, Richard. The doctor committed an illegal act against the patient's will."

"That's what's gonna be hard to prove."

"What?"

"It's a he-said, she-said. Patient says the doctor acted against her will, doctor says he didn't."

"Did you read the case?"

"Of course I read the case. It was a breech birth with complications."

"It was a breech birth with tangled umbilical cord. A cesarean was not only indicated, it was imperative."

"Says who?"

"Says me and the whole damn AMA. If you can find one doctor who says a cesarean shouldn't be performed under those circumstances, I'll buy you dinner."

"Hey, I'm a lawyer. I can find a doctor who'll say anything. And this doctor will say there was no indication of fetal distress until the baby was delivered."

"How do you know that? You haven't even taken his statement."

Richard smiled. "Because any doctor crooked enough to withhold a cesarean under those circumstances is certainly crooked enough to lie about it. If I understand your scribbled notes correctly, the doctor didn't perform a cesarean because he was prevailed upon by a friend of his not to."

"That's right."

"Because his friend was a producer who wanted to use the woman in porn flicks."

"Not porn. Skin flicks. Soft-core."

"Doesn't matter. The attorney for the defendant will say she's a porn actress, and I'll be in the embarrassing position of having to point out the difference. Then we'll have a he-said, she-said between an accredited physician and a welfare mother who acts in sex films."

"There were nurses involved."

"Sure. Who want to keep their jobs. Who should they align themselves with? Gee, I'm a registered nurse. What's my best strategy? Keep my mouth shut and pretend nothing happened, or testify against a reputable surgeon and get transferred to another hospital where no one wants to work with a tattletale? Stanley, you see the world through rose-colored glasses. That are half full. I'm not a do-gooder, a white knight on a steed, a crusading attorney attempting to right the wrongs of the world. I'm out to make money. You know my ads on TV? They're not free. They have to pay for themselves by bringing in enough business to make it worthwhile. I'm sorry if that offends you, but it also pays you."

"But—"

"Doctors pay a fortune in malpractice insurance. You know what that means? That means they don't have to settle. That means they can afford to fight. If I go after a doctor, I want to have the goods."

"You file a zillion trip-and-falls."

"Sure. They're automatic. They're either settled or dropped. It's a no-lose situation. No one's gonna fault you for filing a trip-and-fall that doesn't pan out. Medical malpractice is something else. You get a reputation for filing bogus malpractice claims, it hurts your credibility. I don't want to lose in court. I want opposing counsel to know if I take it, it's sound."

"Are you saying you won't do a medical malpractice?"

"Bring me something to go on. But the unsubstantiated word of the plaintiff? No way."

"There is a dead kid involved."

"Yeah. And the jurors will be sobbing. And probably the

defense attorney. And the doctor may work up a tear. It's a really sad situation. Too bad these things happen. Sometimes it's just unavoidable. Stanley, you wanna pursue this, let me give you some advice."

"What's that?"

"Get a law degree."

14

MACAULLIF'S ATTITUDE HAD CHANGED. It was subtle, but it was there. Oh, he was still his same old sarcastic self, but I could tell he was taking the matter seriously. I wondered why.

"So," he said. "You got a third name for me?"

"Not just yet."

"Too bad. I'm having such fun doing your work, I barely have time to think about mine."

"I assume you were able to trace the name?"

"Oh, you assume that, do you?"

I shrugged. "I doubt if you'd be acting like such an asshole if you had to admit you couldn't do it."

MacAullif ignored the jibe. "Where did you get this name?"

"Victor Marsden?"

"No, Pinocchio. Hey, not bad. I pulled that off the top of my head, but that's the one whose nose grows, right? When he lies."

"I didn't lie to you, MacAullif."

"You didn't tell me the truth, either."

"What do you mean?"

"Didn't you make Victor Marsden out to be the lamb to the slaughter? Wasn't that the impression I got?"

"I think I was very clear not to—"

"Oh, bullshit! We both know what you were very clear about. Not making a definite statement that would put yourself on the hook. But you know and I know you indicated this Victor Marsden would be the whackee, not the whacker."

"You got a problem with that?"

"Only if it isn't true."

"MacAullif—"

"You give me one name. It turns out to be bullshit. Then you give me the real name. Only you can't just *give* me the real name, you have to wrap it in some fine layers of bullshit so it looks like something else."

"I don't know what you're talking about."

"Do you know who Victor Marsden is?"

"No. That's why I asked you to check him out."

"Nice guy. Sends me right into it without any warning."

"Right into what?"

"Victor Marsden is connected to the mob."

"What!"

"With ties to Tony Fusilli. With priors dating back to 1990. For everything from assault and battery to attempted murder." My mouth fell open. "You mean . . . ?"

"There's every indication Victor Marsden is a button man for the mob."

I snapped my fingers. "Button man."

"What?"

"Nothing."

"So, you're right. The guy's a hitman. Why you had me run a schoolteacher first is beyond me. I don't know why you had to dance around the subject so much, but there you are. Your instincts are absolutely right. This is a bad dude. You should stay away."

I took a breath. "Listen, MacAullif."

He put up his hand. "No. You listen. I've listened entirely too much already, and I don't like what I've heard. So you listen to me. I don't know what kind of a game you're running, and I don't want to know. But I do know this: Victor Marsden is not the kind of guy you want to be involved with. Victor Marsden is pond scum. Victor Marsden is living poison. Victor Marsden is the kiss of death. If you've been approached by Victor Marsden to do anything short of buying Girl Scout cookies, say no. I would even pass on the cookies. Get this guy out of your life as fast as is humanly possible. And, please, under no circumstances, ever mention him to me again. Is that clear?"

It was clear. Totally inaccurate, but clear. There was no way to tell MacAullif he had everything upside down. Even if he hadn't expressly forbidden me to do it. There was no hypothetical in the world that could even come close.

I wasn't involved with Victor Marsden. Not directly. Because Victor Marsden wasn't the hitman. Victor Marsden was the mark, the hittee, the intended victim. The innocent, candy-ass schoolteacher MacAullif thought I was yanking his chain about was the actual hitman.

And I was no closer than ever to knowing whether I should take this case. Which I'd already taken. What MacAullif had told me only deepened my moral dilemma. The person Kessler intended to kill was himself a heartless killer. Did that make him any less worthy of being kept alive? One would think it would, in the general scheme of things. Or, in other words, should I really risk what I was risking to save his life?

What *was* I risking to save his life? Would he even know I was saving it? Or would he assume, not knowing me, that I was on the other side? That I, like Kessler, had been hired to take him out?

While Kessler might be up to dealing with such happenstance, I sure wasn't. And wouldn't it be ironic to be killed by the man I was trying to protect?

Should I quit?

Maybe so, but how? I didn't have Kessler's phone number. Even if I did, he wasn't home, he was in class. He probably had a cell phone, but, of course, I didn't have the number. That would have been too convenient. So, if I was going to quit, I'd have to do it in person. And how could I do it in person when I wasn't supposed to contact him.

I had no idea. But I had to figure it out fast.

I was tailing him at four fifteen.

15

HE STOOD ME UP. WHICH would have been bad enough even if Alice hadn't predicted it. Since she had, it was the absolute worst. Not only was someone getting whacked, but my wife was going to blame me for it.

The one saving grace was that the whackee was a less than desirable person. This was no Boy Scout leader, model citizen, employee of the month. This was a button man. A hitter, a shooter, a shitter. A whacker. Plus other dubious designations too numerous to mention. No one was going to weep because Victor Marsden sleeps with the fishes.

That thought led to another. Where would the hit go down? I knew it wouldn't be Victor's apartment. Kessler had assured me that much. And, while I tended to take his assertions with a grain of salt, particularly since he'd stood me up, that was one I figured I could take to the bank. His point about the doorman seeing him tipped the scale. Self-interest is a big motivator. The hit wouldn't go down at home. Where would it, I wondered, as four o'clock gave way to four thirty, too long to blame the no-show on any traffic jam, see-me-after-class, PTA meeting, or whatever. No, I'd been stood up good and proper.

I was contemplating all that when my beeper went off. I have a cell phone, but Wendy/Janet doesn't have the number, because I won't give it to her. She beeps me, same as ever. But I have the phone to call in.

I did, and Wendy/Janet told me to call MacAullif.

That couldn't be good.

It wasn't.

"You know the deep shit you were trying to get out of?" MacAullif said.

"Yeah?"

"You're in it."

"Don't tell me."

"Got a homicide. East Eighty-ninth Street."

"Shit."

"Name of Victor Marsden. Small-time button man for the mob. Ordinarily, no one would give a shit about a guy like that getting whacked. Except . . ."

"Aw, hell."

"I'm asking about him just this morning. Poor timing, don't you think?"

"MacAullif—"

"A Detective Crowley caught the case. Young hotshot, looking to make a name for himself. No respect for his elders, you know what I mean?"

"What did you tell him?"

"I got the name out of a fortune cookie. I took my wife to this Chinese restaurant, at the end of the meal the waitress comes around—"

"MacAullif."

"I gotta bring you in. I hate it like hell, but I got no choice. I got caught with my hand in the cookie jar. Only it's your hand. The fact you were trying to prevent this will be a mitigating circumstance."

"Oh, hell."

"So I'm bringing you in. Where are you?"

"At my office."

"I'll come to you. Be downstairs in ten minutes."

Oh, my god! This was worse than Alice saying I told you so. This was Alice slipping me packs of cigarettes to barter with the other inmates for my safety.

I whipped out my cell phone, called Richard.

"Rosenberg and Stone," Wendy/Janet said.

"It's Stanley. Get me Richard."

"He's on another line. Can I take a message?"

"No, you can't. It's an emergency. Get him *now*."

She didn't argue that much. I guess I sounded frantic.

Richard came on the line a moment later. "This better be damn important."

"The hitman did it."

"Killed the mark?"

"Yup."

"Oops."

"Is that your professional opinion?"

"Are there any details I should know?"

"MacAullif investigated the decedent at my request just this morning."

"Oops."

"And the young stud in charge of the case leaned on MacAullif to bring me in."

"Yikes."

"Do I need an attorney?"

"You might. Let me think if I know one."

"Richard—"

"I'm not a criminal attorney."

"I thought you liked homicide cases."

"I like representing *defendants*. Not pain-in-the-ass, meddling incompetents. I got a client on the other line. You get charged with this thing, give me a call."

A black sedan fishtailed to a stop as close to my feet as it could come without actually running them over. I was about to curse out the driver when MacAullif growled, "Hop in."

I climbed into the passenger seat of the unmarked police car. MacAullif almost let me close the door before he took off.

I righted myself, said, "Where we going?"

"Crime scene."

"How come?"

"Detective Crowley wants to talk to you."

"You turned me in?"

"I had to tell what I knew."

"You turned me in?"

"If you want to think of it that way."

"You turned me in?"

"All right, I turned you in. What was I supposed to do, make up some bullshit story why I wanted to know about the guy?"

"Works for me."

"Of course it works for you. You did it to begin with."

"I told you *exactly* what I wanted."

"You told me he was a hitman."

"I told you he was the mark. *You* told *me* he was a hitman."

"You're quibbling over words."

"Yeah. The words are *killer* and *victim*."

MacAullif swerved around a taxi, cursed at the driver. "Let me see if I've got this straight. Your story now is you knew this guy was going to get killed?"

"That's not what I said."

"Then what's this *killer* and *mark* bullshit?"

I said nothing, let MacAullif concentrate on his driving. He cut off a bus.

"When you answer questions for this hotshot detective, try to remember he's not me. If you feed him your usual bullshit, he's apt to lock you up."

"Thanks for the tip."

MacAullif pulled up in front of the apartment building, where an inordinate number of police cars seemed to be parked. We got out of the car, and he prodded me into the lobby as if I was his collar.

Two uniformed cops hanging out by the front desk seemed to get that idea.

"Who's the perp?" the chubbier one said.

I wanted to fix him with a steely gaze but figured I'd just come off like an ex-con.

MacAullif ignored the comment. "Where's Detective Crowley?"

The thinner uniform jerked his thumb. "Up at the crime scene."

The elevator dinged and two men got off. One was Detective Crowley. I'd never seen him before, but I knew at a glance. He had *plainclothes cop* written all over him. And the look he gave MacAullif was far from impersonal. It was almost as bad as the glare he gave me.

The guy with him was the doorman who'd been on last night. His eyes widened, his mouth fell open, and he pointed his finger.

"That's him!" he said. "That's Rollo Tomassi!"

16

CROWLEY TOOK ME DOWNTOWN. I wasn't exactly under arrest, but I wasn't exactly not under arrest, either. In British detective fiction, I would be "assisting the police with their inquiries." The way I understand it, the alternative to assisting the police with their inquiries is not assisting the police with their inquiries while locked in a cell.

I intended to talk. If that violated detective-client privilege, that was too damn bad. Kessler hadn't leveled with me. He had used me for his own entertainment. Why, I had no idea. But the guy had never wanted me to stop him at all. And I hadn't done it. Unless my phone call from the front desk had done the trick last night, buying the mark a whopping twenty extra hours of life, until he decided to outfox me this afternoon.

Not that it had taken much. Considering, as Alice had pointed out, that the guy was picking me up, instead of the other way around, my effectiveness as a deterrent actually hinged entirely on nothing more binding than Kessler's promise not to do it.

In killing the mark, Kessler had broken his word. And how was I to have prevented that? Should I have disobeyed his orders, staked out his school, followed him from there to my office to make sure he actually came? Maybe that was the leap of logic I should have taken. That if I was to protect Kessler from himself, I would have to disobey his orders. As I had last night when I hadn't taken the hint to go back the office. That had worked. Should I have learned from that? Should I have said, screw the assignment, I'm acting on my own? The thoughts tormented me.

So did Detective Crowley. Who had a lot of questions. And no one seemed to want to protect me from him. Not MacAullif, who was excluded from the interview. Not Richard, who I hoped would look out for my rights.

"Are you under arrest?" Richard asked.

"Not really."

"Call me when you are."

That left me with Detective Crowley. MacAullif hadn't exaggerated in describing him as a young hotshot. He looked barely old enough to vote. I had to remind myself that just because he's young doesn't mean he isn't dangerous.

Crowley came into the interrogation room, sat at the table, and smiled. An endearing, boyish smile. You had to look close to see the hard edge. "Sorry to keep you waiting. I understand you can be of some help."

It was such a cordial greeting it was hard not to reply in kind. "What do you need?"

"I need your story. I understand you may have had contact with someone who may have had something to do with the death of Mr. Marsden."

"Your words, not mine."

He kept the smile on his face, but his eyes narrowed slightly. "Excuse me?"

"I'm not accusing anyone of anything. And I wouldn't want to be put in the position where anyone might get the impression that I had."

"Do you see a stenographer here? No one's going to quote you. I just want to know what happened."

"You're not recording this conversation?"

There was a flick of annoyance before he smiled. "We're just talking. The way I understand it, the victim approached you with the offer of employment."

"Then you understand incorrectly."

"That's not the case?"

"No, it's not."

"And if Sergeant MacAullif states that he ran the victim's name and came up with a notorious hitman for the mob, and the reason you had him run the name was because you'd been employed by this person and felt uneasy about it, that would be incorrect?"

"There are a number of points to that statement, but, on the whole, it would be incorrect."

"Oh, yeah?"

"Yeah."

"All right," Crowley said. "I'd like to speed this along. You haven't been read your rights, and nothing you say can be used in evidence against you."

"Can it be used in evidence against MacAullif?"

That shook him for a moment. He recovered, said, "This isn't being taken down."

"I told MacAullif nothing. We had a few hypothetical conversations."

"About Victor Marsden?"

"Is that the decedent?"

"Don't you know?"

"I only know what I hear. Which isn't always reliable. You tell me Victor Marsden's dead, I'd be inclined to believe you."

"Victor Marsden's dead."

"Are you sure?"

"I saw the body."

"How did he die?"

Crowley frowned. It had to be all he could do not to say, "I'm asking the questions here." He restrained himself, said, "He was shot."

"Where?"

"In the bedroom."

I opened my mouth.

He grinned like a schoolboy. "Couldn't resist. He was shot in the head. One shot, bam, center of the forehead, dropped like a rock. Killer was a pro, knew exactly what he was doing."

"When was he killed?"

Crowley cocked his head. "You need my help in solving this crime?"

"No, but you can make me feel better."

"Excuse me?"

"If anything I did indirectly caused this guy's death, I'd like to know it."

"So would I. What *did* you do?"

"Isn't this where that Miranda warning would come in?"

"I already know what you did from MacAullif. Only his version is all hypotheticals and guesswork. Be nice to get the straight goods."

"Why *isn't* this being taken down?" I asked.

He shrugged. "No reason. We just like to know what you're going to say before you say it."

"What did MacAullif tell you?"

"You had him run two phone numbers. One was an English teacher from Harmon High. The other was a hitman for the mob. No sooner does he run the hitman's record, when the guy gets rubbed out. That alone would be enough to put you on the hook, even if you hadn't been posing as Rollo Tomassi."

"I can explain that."

"Feel free."

"It's from *L.A. Confidential.*"

"I know the reference. Why did you use it?"

"I wanted to shake the guy up. I thought if he knew the reference, that would do it."

"And why did you want to shake the guy up?"

"So something like this wouldn't happen."

"What made you think it would?"

"We're getting into areas here where I might need an attorney."

"You have the right to an attorney."

"Was that a Miranda?"

"Oh, for Christ's sake. This is a conversation."

"Yeah, only you say later, 'I *told* him he had the right to an attorney.'"

"You're being awful cagy. Who you trying to protect?"

"Me."

"What have you done wrong?"

"I haven't done a damn thing wrong."

"Then you got nothing to worry about."

"Tell it to some guy who's served twenty or thirty years in jail before being cleared by DNA."

"Let me help you out here. The way I understand it, you were hired by this hitman, Victor Marsden. Last night you observed him in the company of another man who went up to his apartment. You left shortly thereafter. Sometime today, late morning or early afternoon, the gentleman returned and rubbed out the hitman."

"Without being seen?"

Crowley was only human. He couldn't hold out any longer. "Why am I the one providing all the information? Yeah, without being seen. Which is why we put it between twelve and one, even before we get the medical report. That's the time the doorman goes to lunch and the janitor fills in. It's summer, the regulars take their vacations, most of these guys are replacement temps. Anyone with the balls to flash 'em a smile and stride right to the elevator as if they live there could go right up. I would expect a hitman to have fairly big balls."

"Good point."

"Thank you. Now then. A hitman hired you. Someone killed him. That would seem to terminate the employment. Wouldn't you like to know who did it?"

I sighed. What a mess. Crowley was going on MacAullif's mis-interpretation of the hypotheticals I'd given him. As a result, he had next to nothing right. And I had no way to correct him without sticking my neck in a noose.

I wondered if it was time to barter for immunity.

"What about the teacher?" I said.

"What about him?"

"Have you checked out the schoolteacher?"

"Yes, of course. The schoolteacher is a schoolteacher with an unblemished record. Why you chose him as a red herring is your business. I'm sure you had a reason. Not that I care."

"You might want to give him a second look."

I don't know why I said that. I suppose it was vindictive. I was pissed off at being deceived, and couldn't bear to see Kessler get away scot-free. While that was certainly true, it wasn't good enough. I could secretly want that to happen, but that was a far cry from *making* it happen. From giving up my client. From telling on the guy. It really went against the grain.

And yet I'd done it.

It was like a knife in the gut to realize why.

Crowley wasn't that much older than my son, Tommie. I was feeling paternal toward the boy.

Not that he seemed inclined to accept my help. "I think we can rule the schoolteacher out."

I gawked. "Rule him *out*?"

"Yeah. Why?"

"Let me be sure I understand this. You're not taking the teacher seriously because he has no record?"

"And because he has an alibi. He was teaching school when the hit went down. Makes it hard to consider him a serious candidate."

"Has the doorman had a look at him?"

"Why?"

"To see if he was the guy who was with the decedent last night."

Crowley's eyes narrowed. "Why are you pushing this?"

"I'm not pushing it. I'm just trying to see how you conduct your investigation."

"Well, you be sure and let me know if I'm doing okay," Crowley said ironically.

"You're not even close," I told him. "You're pushing your own agenda, you're asking questions and not paying attention to the answers, and you're ignoring useful information if it doesn't fit with your own, preconceived notion of the crime. Aside from that, you're doing great."

Crowley had had enough. He frowned, regarded me as if I were something to be scraped off his shoe.

"Okay, let's do it the hard way."

17

THE STENOGRAPHER WAS SLOW. I've never had a slow one
before. Usually, speed is one of the abilities they're hired for. This
woman, who couldn't have weighed more than a broom straw,
attempted to make up for it with an irritatingly ponderous manner.
Her notes were scrawled in a meaty hand. She asked for repetitions
in a booming voice. She scowled more frown lines than face. I got
the impression the cops would have fired her if they weren't afraid
of her.

"What was the charge again?" she demanded.

"Obstruction of justice."

"You're accusing me of obstruction of justice?" I said.

"I'm *not* accusing you of obstruction of justice."

"Could you stop saying *obstruction of justice*," the stenographer
complained.

"Abbreviate it."

"Huh?"

"O.J."

"You'll get her confused with the Simpson trial," I suggested.

Crowley took a ten-minute break, came back with a stenographer who could write. I'm sure the other one wasn't fired. Probably promoted.

"All right," Crowley said. "Investigation into the death of Victor Marsden. Interrogation of the witness, Stanley Hastings. He has been read his rights and declined to have a lawyer present."

"I didn't decline to have a lawyer present. I called my lawyer, he didn't want to come."

"So you're waiving your right to an attorney?"

"I'm not waiving anything. I have the right to an attorney at any time in this proceedings. If you ask me a question I don't like, I'm going to get one."

"With regard to the decedent, Victor Marsden, of East Eighty-ninth Street, have you ever been to that address?"

"Let me clear about this. I've never been to Victor Marsden's apartment. I've been to that apartment *building*. I was there last night."

"What were you doing there?"

"I observed the decedent in the company of another man go up in the elevator. I approached the doorman, said I recognized the tenant, wasn't he so-and-so."

"Wasn't he who?"

"I don't remember what name I gave him. It wasn't important. I made it up."

"Why?"

"To get the name of the tenant."

"Did it work?"

"Yes. The doorman said, no, that's not him, that's Victor Marsden."

"And what did that tell you?"

"The doorman wasn't very bright."

"What did you do then?"

"I asked him to call upstairs, see if the guy with him was so-and-so." I saw no need to point out I hadn't thought to do that until the doorman suggested it. Particularly after impugning his intellect.

"He did so?"

"Yes."

"What name did you give?"

We went through the whole Rollo Tomassi thing again. Thank god the first stenographer wasn't there. It would have taken longer than the movie.

"And why did you do that?" Detective Crowley asked.

"Here you are inquiring about things which have no bearing on the case, but which, if construed injudiciously, might tend to cast my actions in an unfavorable light. I therefore refuse to answer."

"You're not a lawyer."

"You won't let me *have* a lawyer."

"I *will* let you have a lawyer."

"My *lawyer* won't let me have a lawyer."

Crowley rubbed his brow. "MacAullif said you'd give me a headache."

"I'm not giving you anything. I'm trying to help you without forfeiting my rights."

"How do you intend to do that?"

"Well, just a hint, ask for facts, not motivations. Ask me what I did, not my state of mind."

"Okay. Did you accept employment from Victor Marsden?"

"No."

"*No?*"

"No."

"MacAullif says you did."

"I am not responsible for what MacAullif says."

"Are you saying MacAullif is wrong?"

"I'm saying MacAullif has no foundation to make such a statement. I'm sure I never made such a statement to him."

"Why would he lie?"

Oops.

"Hang on here. I'm not saying he lied. It's entirely possible he was mistaken."

"How could he be mistaken?"

"You're now asking me for *MacAullif's* state of mind?"

"You're the one who said he might be mistaken."

"I meant it's possible he made an honest error."

"How do you know it's honest?"

"What?"

"Never mind. How do you know it's an error?"

"How do I know anything? You asked me if I was employed by the decedent, Victor Marsden. The answer is no. I don't know the decedent, Victor Marsden. I never met the decedent, Victor Marsden. I had nothing to do with the decedent, Victor Marsden. Anyone who says I did is in error. And that includes MacAullif. MacAullif's an honest cop, so it would be an honest error."

"You blame MacAullif for the situation?"

"I don't blame MacAullif."

"You say he falsely accused you."

"He didn't accuse me of anything."

"Really? He says you were involved with the dead man."

"That's not an accusation."

"Just a simple statement of fact?"

"Just a simple misassumption. As a result of having jumped to a conclusion. Without sufficient evidence to back it up."

"That sounds like bad police work. Are you saying MacAullif's a bad cop?"

"No."

"Are you saying this was *good* police work?"

I sighed. "And you say *I'm* giving *you* a headache."

"You deny you work for Victor Marsden?"

"That's right."

"Who do you work for?"

"Richard Rosenberg."

"Who?"

"Richard Rosenberg, of Rosenberg and Stone. He's the negligence lawyer I work for."

"That's not what I mean and you know it. Who do you work for in this case?"

"I don't work for anyone in this case."

"What?"

"My job is over."

"What was your job?"

"Keeping Victor Marsden alive."

"You were hired to keep a hitman alive?"

"Ironic, isn't it?"

"Who hired you?"

"I don't think I can answer that."

"I'm not playing games here. There's a been a murder. You talk, or I'll charge you with obstruction of justice."

The stenographer never blinked an eye.

"At which point I would have the right to an attorney."

"Except your attorney doesn't want to represent you. Can't say that I blame him."

I said nothing, sat, waited for Crowley to reload.

He did. "Where were you between twelve and one?"

"Oh, please."

"Where were you between twelve and one?"

"I can't remember."

"You can't remember where you were between twelve and one?"

"I can tell you where I *wasn't* between twelve and one."

"Where is that?"

"East Eighty-ninth Street. I wasn't anywhere near East Eighty-ninth Street."

Crowley's eyes narrowed. "You think you may be accused of the crime?"

"No, I don't."

"Yet you go out of you way to deny it."

"Give me a break. You asked me where I was at the time of the murder. I told you I was nowhere near the scene. Does that imply guilty knowledge on my part? No, it implies dumb suspicion on yours."

"You're getting worked up."

"It's somewhat frustrating answering stupid questions that have nothing do with the investigation."

"Oh, I assure you my questions have something to do with the investigation. They may not jibe with *your* theory, but then you're not in charge. To go back to the question you've been evading, where were you between twelve and one?"

"I don't know."

"You don't know?"

"No. It's been a busy day. I've been in Brooklyn and Queens. I stopped in at the office. I stopped in to see Sergeant MacAullif."

"What time was that?"

"What?"

"When you saw MacAullif?"

"I don't know."

"Was it between twelve and one? It was after, wasn't it?"

"I don't know."

"How do you get paid?"

The change of subject threw me. "What?"

"The law firm you work for. How do they pay you? By the job?"

"By the hour."

"Does that include travel time?"

"Of course."

"Let's see your time sheet."

I hesitated.

"I could get a subpoena duces tecum, force you to produce it."

"That would be pretty stupid, don't you think?"

Crowley had a great deal of poise for a youngster. He didn't get mad. He merely waited patiently. Which was harder to deal with than some aggressive prick trying to break me down.

I popped open my briefcase, produced my time sheets.

"Okay," Crowley said. "The case in Brooklyn you put down for two hours. Ditto the one in Queens. If you start at nine, that would take you to one. You had a meeting at the lawyer's, and a meeting with MacAullif. Which came first?"

"The lawyer."

"And that was after you did the cases?"

"That's right."

"Well, say those two cases took you nine to one. Two hours each is an estimate, and probably a generous one. If each case was actually an hour and a half, that would leave you an extra hour. For whatever mischief you might be up to."

"Geez, it's bad enough being accused of a crime without you messing with my time sheets."

"Here's the thing. Say you knock off Brooklyn–Queens in three hours, not four. Well, that leaves you an hour to get into trouble. If you did, I imagine you'd contact your lawyer. If, as you say, he wants nothing to do with it, you might want to contact your police buddy. Only cops don't condone murder. Even when it's a friend."

"Your theory is that on my lunch hour, which I stole from my boss by manipulating my time sheets, I murdered a mob hitman. Then I ran and told my lawyer, who wanted nothing to do with me, so I went and told a cop, who turned me in. Is that what you think I did?"

"No. That's the club I hold over your head to get you to tell what you know. If that doesn't scare you, we throw in the fact your cop buddy's in a lot of trouble for trying to cover for you."

It occurred to me long about then that in attempting to func-
tion as my own attorney I'd been trying to act like a lawyer and
talk like a lawyer instead of thinking like a lawyer. I'd sort of lost
sight of the main object. I asked myself, what would Richard do?

"Am I under arrest?"

"You're just answering questions."

"I'm not under arrest?"

"No."

"Good. Then I'm leaving."

I got up and walked out.

No one stopped me.

18

I staked out Harmon High. First I made damn sure I wasn't being followed. In solving the murder of Victor Marsden, I had one small advantage on the cops. I knew who did it.

It was no use telling Crowley, because he wouldn't believe me. Kessler had no record. Convincing the cops that a professor, whose biggest concern should be grading papers, had just carried out a mob hit was going to be a tough sell.

I needed proof. I didn't know how I was going get it. That wasn't my concern. My main concern was looking the son of a bitch in the eyes and telling him off.

What a prick. The guy didn't need me. I served no useful purpose. Clearly, he intended to go through with the hit all the time. He wasn't even straight with me about not doing it in the apartment. He had lied to me every step of the way, and made sure my employment did no good. What had he needed me for?

Three forty-five and students began streaming out of the school building. Black, white, Hispanic, Asian. Laughing and smoking, and shouting obscenities and bopping to iPods and giving the general impression that any learning that had just transpired was entirely coincidental and not to be inferred.

Scattered among the youth of our nation were a few grown-ups, who tended to fall into two categories: the younger, earnest, and idealistic; the older, jaded, and cynical.

Martin Kessler was not among them. By four o'clock it was clear he had not emerged. I wondered if he had been to school at all.

A couple of black students were having an argument outside the gate. Girlfriend and boyfriend, most likely, from the names they were calling each other, such as *bitch* and *motherfucker.* The girl had her top knotted under her breasts. The boy had the waist of his pants hanging under his ass.

I went over, said, "Excuse me."

The boy said, "Whoa!" and took a big step back. He was lucky he didn't trip on his jeans.

I forgot what I looked like. The kid was probably holding drugs and thought I was a plainclothes cop. I said, "You know Mr. Kessler, the English teacher?"

His eyes were wide. Was this a trick? That was his first assumption. It took a second to realize that would be a mighty strange trick.

"Yeah," he said. "So what?"

"You know him?"

That put him on the defensive again. "I'm in his class. So?"

"Was he in school today? I didn't see him leave."

" 'Scuse me?"

"I didn't see him come out just now. Was he here?"

The girl was either smarter or couldn't resist dumping on him. "Duane, you stupid or what? Man wanna know if the teacher here. He here, but he left."

"When?"

"Enda class. Bell's three forty-five."

"You're saying he taught his afternoon class?"

The girl looked at me the way she'd looked at Duane. "Shee-it."

The two of them were laughing so hard I might as well not have been around. "Where is he?" I interrupted.

"He gone."

"Is there another door?"

She shrugged. "Onliest one I know."

"Any chance he stayed around after school, talked to someone?"

"Man, he *gone*."

I thought that over, and I didn't like it. If Kessler got out of school without me seeing him, that meant he didn't *want* me to see him. Which was understandable under the circumstances. He knew I could stake out his classroom. So avoiding me had to be a short-term goal. Taking pains not to see me now.

While I was thinking that, the teacher most likely to induce passion in students, though not necessarily for her subject, came out. She was dressed conservatively enough, in a loose cotton shirt and mid-calf-length skirt. Her hair was back in a ponytail. She wore large-framed glasses.

Does that describe a raving beauty? No. Quite the opposite. It describes a quite ordinary woman.

Wrong again.

This was a woman to die for. Or to kill for. Even the most unobservant couldn't help but notice that those casual clothes concealed young, perky breasts, with nipples like . . .

But I digress.

Anyway, the girl I'd been talking to saw her and called, "Hey, ma'am. He lookin' for Mr. Kessler."

She flashed a smile. "Just missed him," she said, and kept on going.

It occurred to me, the whole thing could not have been better staged to create the illusion Martin Kessler had been there. What a ridiculous thought. And shame on me for having thought it. These people were not conspirators, sent to play a part. *I'd* approached *them*. The woman wasn't in on it. She'd only said something because the girl said something. A conspiracy theory made absolutely no sense. The only reason I'd come to it was I'd been watching the door, and I was sure Martin Kessler hadn't come out.

Unless . . .

And this is where we start getting into paranoia run wild. I recognized it as such. I knew that's what it was. But somehow that didn't help.

It was a *sound* paranoid thought.

I knew Martin Kessler killed Victor Marsden. I was the *only* one who knew Martin Kessler killed Victor Marsden. I could finger Martin Kessler. I could connect him to the crime. I was a liability, a threat, a serious danger to Martin Kessler, notorious hitman.

I was expendable.

I had to go.

Kessler had snuck out of class today because he was a pro who knew all the tricks of the trade. He spotted me waiting for him, and he avoided me. He avoided me just the way he had avoided the doorman when he had gone in to kill Victor Marsden. He avoided me so he could stalk me. He was probably watching me right now.

My stomach felt hollow. My back tingled like it was in the crosshairs of a high-powered rifle. Or a laser beam, that's what they used now, a tiny pinpoint of light between my shoulder blades, guiding the bullet into my heart. I wouldn't even know it happened. One moment I'd be standing here, the next moment I wouldn't.

Poor Alice.

Would I feel it?

Would I hear it?

I heard it, and I jumped a mile.

19

I AVOID THE MORGUE AS much as possible. Though, in this instance, I wasn't that unhappy to be here. Mostly because I'd walked in of my own accord instead of being carried in feetfirst, which was my expectation when I hear that sound. But, no, it wasn't the whine of a bullet from an assassin's gun; it was merely Wendy/Janet beeping me to tell me to call Detective Crowley. I did, and it turned out he was sending a police cruiser to pick me up. The medical examiner had finished the autopsy, and they wanted me to ID the body. I'm not squeamish, but IDing dead mob hitmen is not my idea of a good time.

"I don't even know the man," I protested.

"You saw him in his apartment building."

"So?"

"In the company of the man who allegedly killed him. We need your ID to put the two together."

"Can't the doorman do that?"

"The doorman doesn't know the man who killed him."

That didn't make sense to me, but then I didn't want it to make sense to me. I wanted to go home, get in bed, pull the blanket up over my head, and pretend this wasn't happening. Maybe that's not heroic, but, excuse me, what would you do, arm yourself and go looking for a hitman from the mob? One with the stealth to get in and out of the apartment building without being spotted. Not to mention a public school. I gotta tell you, I wouldn't like my chances. I know some asshole's always doing it in the movies, but that's a movie. And the asshole presumably has talent. He may be a civilian, but he's brawny, or smart, or some combination of the two, and he has nerves of steel, and never considers the fact he might get killed in his enterprise, because, of course, he doesn't. Sorry, bub, that's not the way it works.

Anyway, it wasn't just the smell of formaldehyde and the harsh flourescent lighting and the cold white marble that was giving me chills.

Crowley noticed. "Never been in a morgue before?"

I ignored the comment. "Where's the damn corpse?"

Crowley jerked his thumb at the wall of pullout drawers they keep the bodies in. "One of these."

"Which one?"

He shrugged. "Shouldn't be a problem. They file 'em alphabetically."

I almost said, "They do?" Thank god, I stopped myself. The image of morticians pulling out drawers, juggling corpses, and making room for new ones was only slightly ludicrous.

"How *do* we find him?" I asked.

"We wait for the ME. Gives me a chance to ask you a couple of questions that are totally off the record. No one here but you and me."

"You're not wearing a wire?"

"You watch a lot of TV?"

"Probably more than I should."

"Then let me give you a hint. If my best shot at solving this was talking to you wearing a wire I'd be a pretty bad cop."

"If you're such a good cop, who did it?"

"I have no idea."

"There you are."

He looked at me narrowly. "You're not still pushing the school-teacher?"

"I'm not pushing anything. I'm just saying if any part of what MacAullif told you was true, it would be in my better interests to get the guy put away before he got the idea I could ID him."

"Are you scared?"

"Of a cold-blooded killer so proficient you haven't got a clue? Why should I be scared?"

"See, that's the other impression you get from the books you read. The idea that the cops are clueless. We're really not so bad."

"Yeah," I said. "Since this thing happened, the only one you managed to pick up is me."

"Funny about that."

A young man in a white coat came into the room. I figured he was a lab assistant, but he turned out to be an ME. I'm really having this age thing lately.

"Who you after?" he asked Crowley. Funny how he pegged him for the detective. We were both in plain clothes.

"Victor Marsden," he said.

"Oh, yeah. Gunshot to the head. Now, where'd we put him?"

The ME looked the drawers over, selected one. "Ah, here we go." He grabbed a handle, pulled it out.

The body slid out just like they do in the movies. Except the sheet was bloody. I hadn't expected that. Blood had oozed from the wound in the forehead where they'd dug out the bullet. Of course, they needed it for evidence to match it up with the gun. Assuming they ever found it.

It was impossible to see the entry wound. It had been sliced open, then sewn up with black thread. I suppose they photographed it a zillion times before cutting in.

I gasped, recoiled.

Crowley smiled at my discomfiture. "Is that the man you saw last night talking with the man you knew as a hitman?"

No, it wasn't.

The man on the slab was the man who'd employed me, the hitman himself, the one who'd given the name of Martin Kessler, a schoolteacher from Harmon High.

20

I DID WHAT THE MORON does in the detective books I read. I held out on the cops. Instead of telling them everything—the sane, normal, sensible course of action—I opted for column B: keep your mouth shut and solve the thing on your own.

Let's not go overboard. I don't think solve-the-thing-on-your-own came into it. It was just that too many realities had suddenly changed for me to make a coherent explanation. If I started talking, I'd still be there. Safely in police custody, but in police custody nonetheless.

Instead, I opted for the short answer. The one that required fewer explanations.

"Yes," I said.

If that gave the police the wrong impression, I'm sorry. But I'm not sure exactly what the right impression was just then.

Richard didn't want to hear it. Which seemed unfair, in light of what happened in the morgue. But he stuck to his guns. "You're not under arrest."

"No, but I lied to the police."

"No, you didn't," Richard said.

"Yes, I did."

"No, you didn't. What a moron. You didn't lie. You made statements which may turn out to be contrary to known facts."

"What's the difference?"

"Three to five."

"Richard."

"Minimum security. Probably get to play golf."

"Richard, I'm in trouble."

"No shit. I'm trying to keep you from getting *me* in trouble."

"Don't you want to get me out?"

"Let's see. I have a lucrative law practice that keeps me in the upper tax brackets. Now, would I want to jeopardize that for a chance of being disbarred and going to jail?"

"Since when were you afraid of the police?"

"I'm not afraid of the police."

A light went on. "You're afraid of the hitman."

"I thought you said the hitman's dead."

"He is."

"Then I'm not afraid of him."

"But you're avoiding the case."

"Yes, I am. Tell you why. You got involved with people who kill people. You weren't smart enough to nip it in the bud, and now it's blown all out of proportion."

"That's how you describe the murder of my client?"

"He's not your client. He's a dead man. You don't work for him anymore."

"But—"

"You should consider the case closed. Whatever money you've been paid, apply it to your fee and write the rest off, because you're not going to see any more."

"What about the murder?"

"What about it? Someone killed your client. That's bad, but the way I understand it, it's better than the other way around. You were afraid your client was going to come after you. He isn't. This other guy doesn't know you, so you're basically out of the picture. You should throw a party."

"To celebrate the fact my client is dead?"

"He wasn't a nice person."

"He seemed like a nice person. He said he was a schoolteacher."

"So he lied to you. A criminal lied. What a shock! No wonder it caught you flat-footed."

"So what do I do about the police?"

"There's nothing you *can* do. You lied to them. All you can do now is compound your lie, or get caught in it."

"Richard—"

"Neither of which is a very attractive alternative. So I would advise you to stay away from the police. *If* I were advising you. Which I'm not. But, if I were, that's the move I would advise you to make. There would be no question in my mind. The only question is, will the police stay away from you?"

"Yeah, but . . . ?"

"Yeah, but what?"

"Everything's upside down. A hitman wants me to stop him from killing somebody. I don't, but somebody else does. By killing *him*. Isn't that a rather unlikely outcome? Doesn't it leave a lot of questions unanswered?"

"Yeah, but they're not your questions. They're a matter for the police."

"I know. But . . ."

"But what?"

"The guy hired me to stop him from killing someone."

"So?"

"Who was I supposed to stop him from killing?"

96

21

I DIDN'T FIND OUT FOR a while because I was off the case. As Richard pointed out, the death of my client more or less ended things. Leaving me no work except his.

I broached the Yolanda Smith case to no avail. Richard had already dropped it. Wondered why I wouldn't let it go.

I wasn't sure myself. I'm not a lawyer. I've never worked for any other lawyer. I wouldn't know who to refer it to. But it struck me as a huge injustice, sitting there like a baseball on a batting tee, waiting for someone to hit a home run.

"It's not just medical malpractice, it's criminal conspiracy. The porn director is in league with the doctor."

"Oh, that'll be fun to prove. Who do I ask, the obstetrician or the auteur?

"You ask 'em both."

"Huh?"

"If they know each other. They deny it, and you prove it, it's a slam dunk after that."

"Oh, is that how it's done? Let me see if I understand this. I subpoena into court two hostile witnesses. Get 'em to lie on the stand. Then I subpoena into court some other hostile witnesses to testify that the first hostile witnesses committed perjury."

"That's unfair."

"What?"

"Calling them hostile witnesses."

"Who?"

"The second ones. The ones testifying the first ones are committing perjury."

"Give me a break. If they know the other two well enough to know that they are committing perjury, they are friends of theirs. Which makes them hostile witnesses. However, you raise a good point. I'll have to *prove* they're hostile witnesses, which I won't be able to do. Not as long as they testify civilly and matter-of-factly, which shouldn't be too hard, as they have no reason to do otherwise."

"You could justify taking this case if you wanted."

"I could justify anything if I wanted. The point is, I don't want. I should think that's abundantly clear."

"The case you *do* want. The quadriplegic. Why do you want that?"

"Are you kidding? It's a *quadriplegic*. It's an injury made in heaven. It's a lawyer's wet dream."

"The woman's baby died."

Richard shook his head. "Sorry. Quadriplegic trumps dead baby every time. The dead baby was never a human being with thoughts, personality, and emotions. He was a nice idea that didn't happen. This is a human being who will be sitting there in court, unable to lift a finger in his own defense. And don't think I won't use that phrase a few times."

"You're not the defense, you're the plaintiff."

"It won't matter. The jurors, if any, will be on his side."

"Why do you say 'if any'?"

"They'll be looking to settle the moment we get to court."

"Then you don't need to go over my testimony."

"Nice try. The point is, this is a case I can win. A simple, straightforward case of a man on whom an egregious injury has been afflicted."

"*Egregious*," I murmured.

"What?"

"Nothing. That's the word that came to mind when I signed Yolanda Smith."

"Forget the woman. Concentrate on the man."

I sighed. "What's the case again?"

"You should know. You signed it."

"When?"

"About six months ago."

"It's coming to trial now?"

"The judge fast-tracked it. On account of the injury."

"I remember signing a quad. Columbia-Presbyterian?"

"That's the one. Recall the case?"

"Refresh my memory."

"Client fell on a broken stair in his apartment building. We assigned you the accident photos the same day. If you'll recall, Wendy beeped you at the hospital, sent you to take them. Instead of waiting for a separate photo assignment . . ."

Richard went on, but I had stopped listening.

A trip-and-fall. That was Richard's egregious case. A trip-and-fall. This is what I'd been pulled in for, given a special photo assignment. This is what I'd have to testify in court. This is what was important, pressing, couldn't be postponed, no matter what my obligation, no matter that a man's life was at stake. This was the case that Richard took, cherished, squandered his talents on. While the truly wronged Yolanda Smith was wronged yet again.

I made a vow, right then and there, if Richard wouldn't help that woman, I would.

Somehow, I'd find a way.

22

"IT'S THE TEACHER," Alice said.

Alice didn't know I was off the case. Well, she did, she just didn't credit it. As far as Alice was concerned, I was off the case when Alice said I was off the case. Which was not likely to happen until it was utterly inconvenient.

"What's the teacher?" I said.

"He's the intended mark."

"How do you figure that?"

"The guy gave you a name. It's not *his* name. But it's *someone's* name. He didn't pull it out of a hat. Why did he give it to you? The only thing that makes sense is that the teacher is the mark."

"Or the hitman."

"What?"

"The *other* hitman. The guy I thought the hitman was following. The guy I thought lived there. The guy I thought was Victor Marsden. What if *he's* the schoolteacher?"

"Is he?"

"I've never seen the schoolteacher. What if he's our guy?"

"I thought MacAullif checked him out and he's clean."

"I'm not putting a lot of faith in MacAullif's investigation."

Alice smiled. "Just because you're mad at him is no reason to demean his abilities. MacAullif's a good cop. If he says he's clean, he's clean."

"He doesn't say he's clean. He just says he doesn't have a record. A careful criminal wouldn't."

"I thought you were watching the school for the guy to come out and he didn't."

"Because he was dead."

"But if the other guy had come out, wouldn't you have recognized him?"

"Oh."

"Though I must admit," Alice said judiciously, "your powers of observation are so poor if the guy was wearing a different jacket it would probably be enough to throw you off."

"Alice—"

"Your theory now is the hitman was hired to kill the schoolteacher, but the schoolteacher turned the tables and killed him?"

"I admit I don't know all the angles."

"There's an understatement."

"But how could I? I was lied to and kept in the dark. All I know is the schoolteacher is important and someone is dead. Isn't he a logical killer?"

"What do the police think?"

"Oh."

"The police don't know what to think because you didn't level with them. If they knew the man you were dealing with was dead, they'd treat the whole matter differently."

"If they knew the man I was dealing with was dead, I'd probably be in jail."

"That's a rather negative way to look at it."

"Alice."

"It's one thing to lie to the cops. It's something else to lie to MacAullif."

"I didn't lie to MacAullif."

"Right. You haven't talked to him because you're mad at him. How long you gonna keep that up?"

We were sitting in the bedroom not watching *House,* the medical show about the sarcastic doctor. Alice and I like *House,* so there's a limit as to how long we can not watch it. That limit is right around fifteen minutes. We have a DVR, the wonderful digital recording system that allows you to pause live TV and start watching a program you're recording at any time. So Alice and I never watch a show when it goes on, we wait at least fifteen minutes so we can zoom through the commercials.

"It's not that simple," I told Alice.

"What do you mean?"

"Straightening MacAullif out wouldn't be doing him any favors."

"You mean he'd have to lie?"

"That's one possibility."

"You mean he'd turn you in? Is that where you're at? He talked to the cops, and you're afraid he'd do it again?"

"I don't know what he'd do."

"I don't either, but he wouldn't hang you; he likes you. Why, I can't imagine."

"You're taking this awfully well, Alice. Considering you're aiding and abetting a fugitive from the law."

"Are you really a fugitive from the law? You're not wanted for anything. True, it's because you lied your way out of it. But, technically, I don't think you're a fugitive."

"Alice—"

"Okay, you want me to say it? I'm glad he's dead. He was your client, and he seemed like a nice guy, and all that. The bottom line is he killed people. He had a record. Not under the name he gave you, but under his own name. He had the record of the type of person you wouldn't deal with. Which is why he gave you someone else's name. He knew you'd check him out. He knew if you saw his record, you wouldn't deal with him. He wanted you to deal with him. Why, I have no idea. But he gave you the name of this schoolteacher. Doesn't it make sense that this schoolteacher is actually the guy he was going to kill?"

"No, it doesn't. Why would anyone want to kill some poor English lit teacher?"

"Exactly," Alice said.

"Huh?"

"He *didn't* want to kill him. He wanted to be *stopped* from killing him. If the mark was some slimy mob type, why would he care? On the other hand, if the mark is some respectable high school teacher with a wife and kids who never harmed a fly, it makes sense he wouldn't want to take him out."

"If the schoolteacher never harmed a fly, why is the hitman *supposed* to take him out?"

"How should I know? I don't know any of the facts of the case. You didn't even tell me the name of your client until he was dead."

"I didn't even *know* the name of my client until he was dead."

"I mean the name he gave you. The high school teacher. The one who's in danger."

"He's not in danger."

"I certainly hope not. Because you've taken it on yourself to look out for his well-being. By not letting the cops in on the story. All they know is you asked MacAullif to trace his name."

"What do you want me to do?"

"I don't want you to do anything. It's just I know you. You carry the weight of the world on your shoulders. If something goes wrong, you blame yourself for it. Even if you had nothing to do with it. This is different. You *are* responsible. You've got information no one else does. If something happens to this guy, you'll never forgive yourself."

23

I TURNED DOWN A CASE in Harlem. Wendy/Janet had a cow, but I stuck to my guns. It was two thirty, and there was no way I'd get done in time to get back to Harmon High.

I was going on Alice's assertion that Martin Kessler was the mark. I didn't believe it for a minute, but I was listening to Alice because I always listen to Alice, because when I don't listen to Alice things go wrong. I get in trouble for not listening to Alice. And not just with Alice. I get in trouble in general. I hate trouble, and I love Alice, so listening to Alice always turns out to be the path of least resistance.

I was on that path encountering little resistance as I camped out in front of the entrance of Harmon High again. Only this time I was not on the lookout for anyone I knew. Unless Martin Kessler turned out to be the fellow I thought was Victor Marsden, the man who presumably killed him. But that didn't seem very likely, since that was *my* theory. And, as Alice had pointed out, not a very good one. Not that hers was any better. Still.

Assuming I was wrong, always a safe assumption, how the hell was I going to identify Martin Kessler? It wasn't like he'd know me. The two of us had never met.

It occurred to me what I needed was a little sign, like chauffeurs hold up at the airport. Yeah, that's the ticket. Stand there with a sign MARTIN KESSLER. Wouldn't be at all conspicuous. No one would know.

So what was I going to do?

While I was stewing about it, I spotted the two kids from the day before. The ones who'd mistaken me for a cop. I wondered if they still thought I was.

I whistled, crooked my finger. "Come here."

From the look on the guy's face, he was holding again. You'd think he'd have learned. If I didn't bust him before, I wasn't gonna bust him now. Nonetheless, he was mighty reluctant.

"Yeah," I said. "You remember me. I was looking for Martin Kessler. Guess what? He never showed."

The look on the kid's face was priceless. "Hey, not my fault, man. How should I know what he did?"

"No way you could know. But the fact is, I missed him. So I still need help."

"Hey, man. I done all I could."

"I'm not saying you didn't. But here's an opportunity to do a little more. Has he left yet?"

He shrugged, but the girl said, "No."

He looked at her. "How you know that?"

"Same way you do. He asked Beez to stay after class. So you know he's talkin' to Beez."

"Yeah. Tha's right. He still there," the kid reported back to me, as if he should get points for the information.

I was ready to give it. "Excellent. Then you can help me. I still won't be able to recognize this guy. So, if you'll stick around until he gets finished with Beez, you can point him out."

He face fell. "Ah, geez."

"In return for which," I went on, "I will give you twenty bucks." I waggled my finger in the direction of the girl. "And the two of you can go to the flicks."

"Flicks?"

"The movies. Don't they say *flicks* anymore?"

"Movie's ten seventy-five," he groused.

"Okay. I will give you twenty-one dollars and fifty cents."

"Imax is more."

I couldn't believe I was bargaining with the kid. "The size of the screen is your problem. I'm paying twenty-one fifty."

"I gotta introduce you?"

"No, just point him out."

"He gonna see me do it?"

I suppressed a smile. The kid didn't want to take the responsibility for fingering his teacher. "He doesn't have to know it was you. Just point him out, and slip away."

"You bustin' him?"

"Duane!"

"I gotta know."

"No, I'm not busting him."

"No one's gonna get hurt?"

"No one's gonna get hurt."

He crossed to the uptown side of the street, walked about fifty feet west, and stopped behind a parked car. The girl and I followed. From there we had an excellent look at anyone coming out the front door. Obviously, the kid had used this vantage point before.

"Where's the money?"

I took a twenty out of my wallet, fished a dollar fifty out of my pants. I had visions of him taking it and running. Clearly he wasn't about to. After all, I still might be a cop.

We settled down to wait. While we did, it occurred to me I had been somewhat cavalier in assuring Duane no one was going to get hurt. After all, someone was already dead.

"Tha's him," Duane said, pointing at the schoolhouse door.

Martin Kessler was a perfectly ordinary-looking young man, maybe thirty-five to forty. His brown hair was shorter than your average rock star, longer than your average drill sergeant. He wore a jacket and tie, though his shirt was open at the collar. With horn-rimmed glasses, he could have passed for a tax accountant. My mind kept turning backflips. He's not a teacher. He's a bookkeeper for the mob. He's being rubbed out because he knows too much. An unlikely scenario, but still more likely than the one where he's a hitman for the mob who rubbed out Victor Marsden.

At least he wasn't the guy I'd seen with my client. The guy I suspected of killing my client. He was someone else entirely. I didn't know whether to find that reassuring or decidedly unhelpful.

At any rate, my snitch and his henchwoman snuck off after fingering the English lit prof, leaving me to my own devices.

The smart thing would have been walk up to the guy and introduce myself. But why should I start doing the smart thing now? Instead, I hung back in the shadows to see where he'd go.

He headed for Broadway, which was fine by me. I followed him from the north side of the street. I've never tailed an English lit teacher before, but I think I did a pretty good job.

I followed him to Broadway, caught the subway downtown. All right, maybe it was stupid, but I did actually have a purpose in mind. I wanted to see if anyone else was taking any interest in him.

Apparently no one was. I didn't know whether to be disappointed or relieved. On the one hand, it made for awfully dull surveillance. On the other hand, dull was just about my speed.

Kessler took the subway to Forty-second Street, transferred to the Shuttle. I went in the door at the other end of the car. I doubt if he'd have noticed me if I'd stood on his feet, but I was taking no chances. No one else seemed interested in Kessler. Of course, it was rush hour, the car was packed, and any number of hitmen could have been sizing up the little professor and laying plans for future eradication without anyone noticing.

107

We shuttled to Grand Central, caught the Lexington Avenue local downtown.

Martin Kessler lived on East Twenty-eighth Street. At least he was going to East Twenty-eighth Street. Whether he actually lived there was another matter. I tried to recall if MacAullif had supplied me with an address. If he had, I didn't remember it.

Kessler walked up the steps of a brownstone between Lexington and Third. It was one of those townhouses divided into apartments. He whipped out of set of keys, opened the front door.

I could have run up to him then, but he probably would have thought he was being mugged. Not that I look like a mugger; still, no one likes to be bearded on his doorstep. I let him go inside, watched to see if anyone else had noticed. No one had.

I sighed.

To warn or not to warn. That is the question.

The answer, of course, is warn. In a situation like that, you always warn. Because, if you warn and the suspect gets killed, you've done all you could. And if you don't, you haven't.

I went up on the stoop. There was a row of buttons marked B, 1, 2, and 3. I assumed B was for basement, though there was a separate outside door.

Button #1 said KESSLER. I pressed it. Moments later a woman's voice said, "Yes?"

I hadn't expected a woman, though Martin Kessler certainly had every right to one. In fact, a wife and kid had been part of Alice's scenario.

"Is Martin Kessler there?"

"Who is it?"

"My name is Stanley Hastings. I have a message for Mr. Kessler. It's rather important."

"Does he know you?"

"We haven't met, but he'll know who I am."

"Marty, do you know a Stanley Hastings?"

"Who?"

I pressed the button, said, "He doesn't know my name."

Moments later a man's voice said, "Who is this?"

"Mr. Kessler?"

"Yes."

"My name is Stanley Hastings. I need to talk to you. It's very important. Do you live on the first floor?"

"Yes."

"Look out the window."

After a moment I saw a face in the window. I stepped out on the sidewalk, executed a pirouette. I went back and pressed the button. "Do I look dangerous to you?"

Wrong question. I looked like a lunatic to him.

I pressed the button again. "Have the police been in touch with you? I bet they have. About a murder you know nothing about. If you're interested, I have some information. I know why they're bothering you."

The door clicked open. The schoolteacher peered out. "Who are you?"

"Stanley Hastings."

"Your name means nothing to me."

"Join the club."

"Huh?"

I flashed my identification. "I'm a private investigator. I happen to know the police interrogated you about the Marsden murder. I have some things I think you should know."

"What?"

"I think you might be in danger."

"Come in."

His living room looked like something an English teacher might inhabit. It was wall-to-wall books, except for the windows in front.

Kessler's wife was an Earth Mother sort, in peasant skirt and blouse. She wore her straight blond hair cut in bangs. Her breasts were large, as if she were nursing. I thought I heard a baby cry in the back room.

"You have children?" I asked.

"Two," he said.

Earth Mother's eyes blazed. "Never mind the small talk. You said we're in danger. At least my husband is. Now, what do you mean by that?"

"What have the police told you?"

"They haven't told us anything. They were investigating a suspicious death, and they wanted to know where Marty was between the hours of such and such. It happened to be a time he was in class. It was obviously a mistake, and they knew it. They told us to forget about it. Now you bring it up again and say we're in danger. Why?"

"All right," I said. "It's not accidental the police got your name. Your name was brought up in connection with the man whose murder they're investigating."

"What do you mean, 'brought up'?"

"It's a delicate matter. There are things I can tell you, and things I can't tell you. But say you were quite deliberately brought into the picture. The question, of course, is why?"

"I'm still not following you."

"Okay, try this on for size. The police had two names. Victor Marsden and Martin Kessler. Victor Marsden is dead. Someone killed him. No one knows why. But it's possible the person who killed him was attempting to kill Martin Kessler. If so, it won't be long before he discovers his mistake."

"You're saying this person might be trying to kill me?"

"That's right."

Martin Kessler's grin was enormous. "That's absolutely idiotic. No one's trying to kill me."

A bullet whizzed by his head and imbedded itself in the wall.

24

I SUPPOSE I COULD HAVE been lucky and not gotten Crowley. After all, this wasn't a homicide. Or even an attempted homicide. It was really just a stray bullet. Which in New York, alas, isn't that rare. Only the timing was unfortunate. My suggestion that the man might be in danger before a bullet missed him by inches had rather nasty implications. At least that's the way his wife seemed to take it. She made no bones about calling the cops. And insisted she talk to someone involved in the Victor Marsden case. Upon which the shit hit the fan.

Crowley wasn't far behind. He settled himself at Kessler's dining room table, accepted the cup of coffee Earth Mother offered him, and sat there sipping it just as if he were a student in one of Kessler's seminars.

"So," Crowley said, "this gentleman nearly got you shot."

It was all I could do not to jump to my defense. But nothing I could say was going to be of any help.

Not that I needed help. Kessler was broad-minded. Magnanimous. "I'm not saying it's his fault, but it's certainly what he had in mind."

"He came to see you?"

"That's right."

"Did he call first? Make an appointment?"

"No. He just rang the bell."

"He rang the bell, you let him in, and almost got shot."

"Not that quickly."

"Well, how quickly was it?"

"I don't know. He was explaining why he was here."

"Why was that?"

"To warn me."

"Warn you of what?"

"He said my life might be in danger."

"Did he now? And why was that?"

"He didn't say."

Crowley looked over where the detective was digging the bullet out of the wall. "I'm going to want to match that up."

The detective had to be a good ten years Crowley's senior. His look said, "Gee, I never would have thought of that."

Crowley turned his attention back to Kessler. "You have no idea why your life might be in danger?"

"Just what he said."

"I thought he didn't say anything."

"Just my name."

"What about your name?"

"He said the police had two names. Mine and another guy's. And the other guy is dead."

Crowley cocked his head ironically. "Did he happen to mention where the police *got* those two names?"

"No. Why?"

"Never mind. Did what he said scare you?"

"No. It sounded stupid."

"What about now?"

"It still sounds stupid. But apparently there's something to it."

"How soon after he entered the apartment did you get shot at?"

"It was only a few minutes."

Earth Mother was getting impatient. "You're asking the wrong question."

"Excuse me?" Crowley said.

"The shot was a few minutes after he entered the apartment. But it was *immediately* after my husband stepped in front of the window."

"Is that right?"

"Yes, it is."

"Why did you go to the window?"

"I didn't go to the window. We were talking. I stepped in front of the window."

"He didn't *suggest* you go in front of the window?"

I kept my mouth shut, but it was getting harder and harder.

"No, he didn't."

"Or *lead* you to the window?"

"He didn't lead me to the window. He may have stepped in front of the window."

"Really? He walked to the window and you followed?"

"That's a little strong."

"But accurate?"

"No, it's not accurate. The three of us were in the room. We were all standing. Countered as people said things."

"Countered?"

Kessler looked embarrassed. "I staged the Christmas pageant. That's theater talk."

"That's ridiculous," Mrs. Kessler said. "Nobody countered anything. Nobody led anybody to the window. This gentleman looked around the room because he'd never been here before. He stepped in front of the window. My husband did, too. And someone shot."

Crowley jerked his thumb in my direction. "Any chance the shot could have been aimed at him?"

"Is that wishful thinking?" I said sarcastically. Still, I found the idea unsettling. Even knowing it wasn't true.

Crowley ignored me and the Earth Mother, concentrated on Kessler. "He never called your attention to the window?"

Kessler hesitated. "Oh."

"Well?"

"I'm an English teacher. The word *never* . . ."

"I don't care if you're the Queen of Sheba. I asked the question because I want an answer. Did he ever direct your attention to the window?"

"Well, that's the thing," Kessler said. "He rang the bell. I didn't know who he was. I was reluctant to let him in. He told me to look out the window."

"He told you to look out the window?"

"That's right."

"You went to the window then?"

"Yes."

"The same window the shot came through?"

"That's right."

"What happened then?"

As Kessler described my dance move, Crowley sized me up from head to toe as if he'd just cracked the case. Of course nothing made sense. The operation was being masterminded by a lunatic.

Crowley cocked his head. "Just for fun, you want to attempt an explanation?"

"I was trying to show him I was harmless. Clearly that backfired."

"And while he was framed in the window—no one shot at him then?"

"No."

"So you had to go inside."

"Yeah," I said sarcastically. "Because I wanted to meet his wife and be standing next to him when he was shot, just in case you missed the implication that I might be involved."

Earth Mother appreciated the logic. "That really doesn't make any sense."

Crowley frowned. "Before you go taking his side, I would like to point out that this man has refused to cooperate with the police. If he had, this could have been prevented."

"Oh, bullshit," I said. "I told you this guy might be in danger. You thought the idea was stupid, so I stopped making suggestions."

"That's not what happened."

Out of the corner of my eye I could see the detective digging the bullet out of the wall was grinning from ear to ear, and clearly getting a kick out of my giving Crowley a hard time.

Crowley noticed. "You got that bullet yet? Make sure you keep track of any scratches *you* put on it."

"That his first bullet?" I said, rubbing it in.

"I'm through playing games." Crowley clapped his hand on Kessler's shoulder. "Do you have reason to believe this man might be in danger?"

"Yes, I do."

"Why?"

"Someone shot at him."

Crowley's face was turning red. "Besides that."

"I traced the names of two people. One of them is dead. That raised concerns for the other."

"Why?"

"Fifty percent is a statistically poor survival rate."

"Who gave you this man's name?"

"My client."

"Really? What did he say about him?"

"He didn't say anything about him."

"He just gave you his name?"

"That's right."

"Why did he give you his name?"

"I can't answer for his motivations."

"Did he ask you to trace it?"

"No, he did not."

"What did he say when he gave you his name?"

"I'm not discussing my business with my client."

"You're not a lawyer. You don't have attorney-client privilege. You can't refuse to answer questions about what your client told you."

"Oh, yeah? Just watch me."

Crowley's mouth fell open. So did Kessler's and the Earth Mother's. The detective kept his cool, but he was enjoying it enormously.

"I'm just an ordinary citizen, but I have rights. You can't push me around. I'm done answering questions, and I'm going home. If you want to detain me, you'll have to arrest me."

"All right, damn it. You're under arrest."

"Well, it's about time."

I whipped out my cell phone, called Rosenberg and Stone.

25

RICHARD ROSENBERG WAS AT HIS sarcastic best. "Let me be sure
I got this straight. You arrested this man because you didn't like the
way he answered your questions?"

"Don't be silly," Crowley said.

"I assure you I'm not being silly. I've listened to your explanation and that's all I can come up with. You don't even seem to have
a charge. To the best I can determine, you arrested my client on
suspicion of not pleasing you with his answers."

"I arrested your client on obstruction of justice."

"Yes, but that's such a broad charge. Barricading yourself inside
a bank, taking hostages, and shooting the negotiator would certainly be an obstruction of justice."

"Don't be ridiculous."

"It's not ridiculous from the point of view of the negotiator."
Richard shrugged. "On the other hand, I assume refusing to pay
your parking ticket could be considered obstruction of justice."

"On the other hand," Crowley countered, "withholding material evidence in a murder case could be considered obstruction of justice."

"Good thing my client hasn't done that."

"Oh, but he has."

"Really? I'd like to see you prove it. I can't wait to get you on the stand."

"Your client accepted employment from a hitman. Knowing he was a hitman. That hitman is now suspected of a murder, and your client won't talk. I don't see where you've got much wiggle room."

"That's because you didn't go to law school." Richard pursed his lips. "Look, here's my best offer. Let us walk out of here right now and I won't make it a matter of principle to wind up with your house and car."

Crowley scowled. "Are you threatening me?"

"Absolutely not. A threat implies the intention to do something wrong. My intention is merely to go to court."

"So, according to you, the phrase 'threat of legal action' has no meaning?"

"Oh, do you want to debate semantics? I love debating semantics at four hundred and fifty bucks an hour. Only I doubt if my client can pay it. I'd have to sue him for my fee."

"I'm not fooling around here. There's been a murder and an attempted murder. Your client's involved."

"In what way?"

"He knows the killer. He was employed by the killer. Now he's covering up for the killer. As well as his own involvement."

"You're saying Stanley's an accessory to murder? As a charge, I like it better than obstruction of justice."

"I'll file it if you don't cooperate."

"Now, that would count as a threat of legal action. You're quite right, there is such a thing, and you're guilty of it."

"I want to know the name of your client."

"Stanley Hastings."

"Not *your* client. *His* client."

Richard grimaced. "There we run into a problem. It is possible that my client's client was not entirely truthful in giving his name. Leaving my client with an erroneous perception of who he actually was."

"Are you saying that's the case?"

"I'm saying it's possible."

"It's possible pigs fly, but I wouldn't want to bet on it."

"Too bad. That would be an interesting wager."

"Are you going to keep evading the question?"

"I'm not evading the question."

"You're not answering it, either."

"You're the one who started talking about pigs."

Richard's cell phone rang. He whipped it out, said, "Hello? . . . Thank you," and flipped it shut. "Judge Harwell has done me the favor of going to court. He is there now for the purpose of fixing bail for Mr. Hastings. Care to take a little stroll? I can't wait to hear the evidence on which you base the current charge. Or the ones you're threatening me with. Judge Harwell's going to love those."

Crowley looked like a naughty schoolboy about to be sent to the principal.

I loved it.

26

RICHARD WASN'T PLEASED, despite getting to flaunt his legal prowess and bop cops around, usually two of his favorite activities. He seemed to enjoy persuading Judge Harwell to release me on my own recognizance, but I guess it wasn't that much of a challenge. The minute we were safely out on the street, he raised a withering eyebrow. "Really, Stanley, this is beneath you."

"You said call if I got arrested."

"For murder. Not obstruction of justice."

"You weren't specific. You're a lawyer. You should have closed that loophole."

"I suppose," Richard groused. "Tell me, did you goad them into arresting you?"

"Just a little."

"Serves me right. So, what's the story with this bullet?"

"You know as much as I do. I called on the guy. Someone shot a bullet."

"Was he tailing you?"

"Who?"

"The guy who shot the bullet. Come on, numbnuts. These questions aren't all that hard."

"I didn't see anyone following me. And I was looking for it. It doesn't mean they weren't. But if I'm right, they went straight for Kessler."

"When's the last time you were right?"

"You'd have to check with my wife. She keeps a list."

"You're sure they were shooting Kessler?"

"I was standing right there."

"No chance they were shooting you?"

"No. Why would they?"

"Because of Kessler. You yourself are not dangerous. But if you get to Kessler, who knows, you might put two and two together."

"Put what together? I haven't got a clue."

"Yes, but the shooter doesn't know that. The shooter may think you're competent."

"Thanks a bunch."

"In which case the shooter may try again. The police will most likely be protecting Martin Kessler. I can't imagine they'd do the same for you."

"No one's after me."

"Are you sure?"

"Trust me. I've been on my guard."

"*You* thought someone might shoot you?"

"No, but . . ."

"But what?"

"Before. When I thought my client was at large. Before I knew he was dead. It occurred to me I was the one who could ID him. Connect him to the crime."

"That would be a worry. Aside from the fact he deliberately put you in that position."

"Right. But he's dead. And I don't know the guy who killed him from Adam."

"No, but you saw the two of them together."

"So did the doorman. Are you saying he's in danger?"

"Maybe, but he's not my client. You wouldn't be either if you hadn't lied to me."

"I didn't lie to you."

"You misrepresented. You told me you'd been arrested. You didn't say it was for littering."

"Accessory to murder doesn't qualify in your book?"

"You're not charged with that. I couldn't even goad them into taking a stab at it. No, I think you're clear until trial."

"Trial?"

"What did you think happened with charges like this? I have to defend you in court. My billable hours should eat up your salary for the next two years. So I'd advise you to go back to work. You got some cases to go out on?"

"You want me to handle cases?"

"What were you planning to do? Curl up and die? You gotta get along with your life. As long as you're doing that, you might as well work for me."

"Swell."

"Just one thing."

"What's that?"

"Watch your back."

27

I GOT IN MY CAR.

A voice from the backseat said, "Drive."

"Jesus Christ, MacAullif."

"Come on. Let's go."

"You got a gun to my head?"

"I wish."

"Hey, who ratted on who?"

"Who ratted on who? Who dumped a steaming pile of bullshit in the middle of whose office and said, 'Have a nice day'?"

"I didn't lie to you, MacAullif."

"Oh, no? Did you tell me the truth?"

"I didn't tell you anything. We discussed a hypothetical situation."

"Yes, and when I'm hypothetically fired and lose my hypothetical pension, that'll be a great solace to me."

"How could they fire a cop who uses words like *solace*?"

"Will you drive, for Chrissakes? I'm really cramped back here."

"Sure. Anything to make you comfortable."

I pulled away from the curb with more force than was actually needed. I didn't leave rubber, but I didn't take that much with me, either.

MacAullif cursed and sat up. I could see his face in the rearview mirror.

"How'd you get my car door open?"

"I'm a cop."

"That's the type of answer that tends to annoy us civilians."

"God forbid I should do that."

"Look, MacAullif, you picked me up, you handed me over to the cops, you said you had no choice. That may be true, but the fact is you did it, and now you're pissed about it."

"At the time I was not aware of certain things."

"What things?"

"Martin Kessler."

"I told you about Martin Kessler."

"You told me dick about Martin Kessler. You had me trace the name Martin Kessler just to show I could trace the name."

"That is not why I had you do it."

"*Now* you tell me."

"Do you really think I'd waste your time making you prove you could trace a name?"

"No. But you'd do it to throw me off the track."

"That's why you turned me in? Because you were mad at me?"

"Don't be stupid. What's all this about the schoolteacher?"

"Someone tried to shoot him."

"Why?"

"Because you traced his name."

"Why did I trace his name?"

"Because I gave it to you."

"Don't be a wiseass. I got a very short fuse on this one."

"Where would you like to go?"

"Downtown is good."

"Wanna get in the front seat?"

"I'm too big to climb in the front seat."

"I'll stop the car."

"You gonna drive off and leave me?"

"You're really paranoid."

"You're really pissed."

"I'm not going to drive off and leave you. I need to know what you know."

"I don't know *anything*. That's why I'm in so much fucking trouble."

I pulled over to the curb. MacAullif got out. He made a show of closing the back door before he opened the front, in case I really did plan to take off. When I didn't, he hopped inside, said, "Let's go."

"Seatbelt."

I pulled out from the curb, blended into traffic. A taxi blared its horn, swerved around me.

"You always drive this badly?"

"What's the matter, MacAullif? You weren't this angry when you dropped me at the crime scene."

"Why should I be? At the time, you only got me involved with a homicide. Could have happened to anyone. Then you got me involved in another shooting with some other bozo whose name I traced. It's a wonder I'm still on the force."

"I didn't shoot at the guy, MacAullif."

"No, but you led the shooter right to him."

"Maybe, but I don't think so."

"That's what I hear."

"Yeah, well, I don't think that's what happened. I think someone took a shot at Kessler, which was the point all along."

"Of course it was," MacAullif said. "Because a hitman walked into your office, gave you the names of two people he intended to kill. He killed one, missed the other. And god forbid you should cooperate with the police."

"I *am* cooperating with the police."

"Yeah. You ID'd the corpse. Who'd already been ID'd by the doorman. That was a big help."

"Oh."

"What?"

"About the ID."

"What *about* the ID? Who *cares* about the ID? There's no *question* about the ID."

"What if there was?"

"Excuse me?"

"Well, hypothetically—"

"I'll kill you. I'll empty my service revolver into your head and stomp on your dead body."

"You want me to say this without a hypothetical? You want me to put you in the position of having to turn me in?"

"I'd be glad to."

"I know."

"Don't talk. Don't say a word." MacAullif took a deep breath, blew it out again. "Is there something wrong with the ID? There *can't* be anything wrong the ID. The guy's been ID'd by separate sources. So what could there be wrong with the ID that would make you have to resort to hypotheticals?" He put his hand in my face. "Don't tell me!"

"Don't worry. I won't."

"You ID'd the corpse as Victor Marsden?"

"He *is* Victor Marsden."

"You didn't ID him as a hitman?"

"He *is* a hitman."

"Is he the hitman who hired you?"

"On the advice of counsel, I cannot comment on anyone, living or dead, who may or may not have hired me."

"Richard make that up?"

"No, I did. Sounds authentic, doesn't it?"

"Sure does." MacAullif frowned. "If your client is dead, why wouldn't you say so?"

"I'm not saying my client's dead."

"Are you saying he's alive?"

"I'm not saying shit. I'm not talking about my client."

"That opens a whole new can of worms."

"I never understood that expression. Who buys cans of worms?"

I hung a left on Chambers Street, headed east.

"If your client's dead, what are you doing in the case?"

"That's a big if."

"If your client's dead, you lied to Crowley."

"I take it that would not be good?"

"Let's see," MacAullif said. "Your license is revoked and you go to jail."

"What's the down side?"

"The down side is I beat you within an inch of your life for doing this to me."

"To you?"

"Oh. Sorry to take it personally, but you had me trace two names, and then lied about the result. Leaving me in the somewhat embarrassing position—"

"Of having to turn me in," I said. "For throwing out a few hypotheticals."

"No. For lighting a time bomb that blew up in my face."

"Hey. I gave you the straight goods. I can't help it if you didn't listen."

"In what way was that the straight goods?"

"I gave you the name Martin Kessler. I insisted it meant something. You insisted it didn't. You'd still be insisting if he hadn't got shot at."

"Hey, douchebag. We all thought Kessler didn't mean anything because you didn't tell us any different. Even though you knew different. So, when you start handing out the raspberries, start with yourself."

"Handing out the raspberries? Is that your dime novel dialogue, MacAullif?"

"So, Kessler didn't mean anything. But he did, because someone shot at him. And Marsden did mean something, because someone killed him. I've been going on the assumption the killer was your client. But if *Marsden* was your client . . ."

"Yeah?"

"Who killed him?"

28

ALICE WAS PREDICTABLY PLEASED. Since everything had blown up in my face, I could count on her to put a good spin on it. "So, you made up with MacAullif. That's nice."

"I didn't make up with MacAullif."

"All right. MacAullif made up with you. Is that better?"

"Alice—"

"I know you men have this whole macho ritual where you can't admit that you're wrong or have any feelings whatsoever. Fine. Be that way. Let me have them for you. MacAullif made up with you, and it's a very good thing. I'm relieved."

"I'm sorry, but you're wrong. MacAullif is still pissed as hell."

"Because you held out on him again?"

"I didn't hold out on him again."

"Did you tell him the dead man was your client?"

"Not exactly."

"What does that mean?"

"I gave him a hypothetical."

"Stanley."

"I think it was damn decent of me giving him anything at all after he went running to the cops."

"Yeah, but he apologized for that."

"He didn't apologize."

"He got in your car. You don't take that as an apology?"

"That was an attempt to get information."

"So, in spite of everything, MacAullif came to you for information. Once again you hit him over the head with a hypothetical."

"Hey, how'd I get to be the bad guy?"

"You went to work for a hitman."

Alice was taking it very well, considering I nearly got shot. Of course, the bullet through Martin Kessler's window had borne out her contention that he was the target. Still, I would think being right was small consolation for losing your husband. Not that that had happened, but you know what I mean. The bullet had come damn close. I would expect a concern for my welfare to outweigh any impulse to gloat.

Not that Alice was gloating. But she couldn't help reminding me now and then how things had turned out.

"We need to think this through," Alice said, which is a euphemism for "You need to listen to my analysis of the situation." Since my own was practically nonexistent, that wasn't such a bad idea.

"Shoot," I said. "Bad choice of words," I amended. "Anyway, go on."

"What do you mean, go on?" Alice said. "I don't know what happened. I'm waiting for you to tell me."

"Tell you what?" I countered.

"All right, let's look at the evidence. Someone tried to shoot the schoolteacher, which makes the schoolteacher look like the mark. If that's true, the hitman deliberately gave you a lead to the schoolteacher because he wanted you to check out the schoolteacher. And protect the schoolteacher."

"Why didn't he just tell me the schoolteacher was the mark?"

"Maybe he didn't trust you."

"He trusted me enough to tell me he was a hitman."

"No," Alice corrected. She raised one finger. "He trusted you enough to tell you *Martin Kessler* was a hitman. You see what I mean? He wasn't trusting you with his *own* identity, *or* the identity of the mark. He was giving you just as much information as he wanted you to have. He gives you Kessler's name for two reasons. One, he wants you to get a lead to him. Two, he knows you'll check him out, and Kessler's record is clean. You check out Martin Kessler, you find a decent guy you'll be willing to work for. You check him out under his own name and you'd turn him down flat."

"That's a little far-fetched."

"Would you have worked for the man identified as Victor Marsden?"

"No," I admitted grudgingly.

Alice smiled. "So, as far as you know, you're working for a schoolteacher named Martin Kessler who kills people in his spare time."

"That's absurd."

"Isn't it? This is where a warning light should go on. Before that can happen, our hitman leads you a merry chase and suddenly you're caught up in playing this game of cops and robbers."

"And what's the point of that? I thought the hitman's purpose was to get me involved with the schoolteacher."

"So?"

"So the surveillance had nothing to do with him."

"How do you know?"

I frowned.

Alice pressed her advantage. "You never saw the schoolteacher in your life. You wouldn't recognize him if he walked up and shook your hand. How do you know all the time you were shadowing the hitman, the hitman wasn't shadowing him?"

"Oh, come on."

"No, think about it. How do you know?"

"Well, for one thing, he picked me up at my office. He wasn't following the schoolteacher. Unless the schoolteacher had a reason to go by my office."

"Maybe he did."

"It would be a hell of a coincidence."

"Would it? It would answer one question."

"What?"

"Why did the hitman choose you? I mean, out of all the detectives in New York, you would certainly seem the unlikeliest."

"Thanks a lot."

"On the other hand, if the guy he's tailing goes by your building every day when he gets off work, he's tailing the guy, he ducks in the doorway, he sees your office listed in the lobby directory. He wants a private eye for this particular job. Here's one right on the way."

"It's still a stretch."

"Why?"

"The schoolteacher doesn't walk downtown. He takes the subway."

"He did today. That doesn't mean he does everyday."

"He teaches at Ninety-second Street. He's not going to walk to Times Square."

"Is that your only objection?"

"You said he walks by my office."

"So?"

"Usually. As a rule. So the hitman can depend on it."

"Just because he didn't do it today doesn't mean it isn't usual."

"Alice, no one walks fifty blocks to get on a train."

"So? What if he takes a bus down Columbus and buys fish for dinner?

"Fish?"

"Some little place around Fiftieth has really good salmon. He takes the bus and buys fish, then walks to the subway and takes the train. Don't you get a free transfer from the bus with your Metrocard?"

"Yeah, but—"

"What's wrong with that?"

"Columbus Avenue is Ninth Avenue. My office is east of Seventh. You don't pass it to get to Times Square."

"You do if the fish market's on Sixth."

"What?"

"He takes the bus down Columbus Avenue, walks across Forty-eighth Street to Sixth Avenue." Alice put up her hand. "I know it's really Avenue of the Americas, but who's going to say all that when they can say Sixth?"

"Alice."

"So, he buys fish on Sixth Avenue between Forty-seventh and Forty-eighth, and walks across Forty-seventh back to Broadway and down to Times Square. He goes right by your office, so that's where the hitman picks you up."

"Yeah, but . . ."

"But what?"

"We weren't following the schoolteacher. We never went near Martin Kessler's apartment."

"Didn't you say you guys went into a movie theater on Forty-second Street?"

"Yeah. So?"

"So maybe the schoolteacher went to the movies."

"With a bag of fish?"

There was no use arguing. Not with Alice. Talk about a futile gesture. "And what is the reason for all this?" I asked. "From the hitman's point of view, I mean?"

"Exactly what he told you. He doesn't want to kill the guy. With you watching, he won't. You do, and he doesn't. So he leads you back to your office, where ninety-nine out of a hundred private eyes would congratulate themselves on a job well done and go home.

"You, of course, refuse to take the broad hint, and tag along. You follow your client home. Naturally, he spots you."

"Naturally."

"Now, don't get offended. The guy is a pro. He'd spot anybody. It's not just you."

"If he spots me, why doesn't he do something about it? Why does he just go home?"

"Ah!" Alice said. "That is where Hitman Number 2 comes in. Hitman Number 1, your hitman, the dead one, picked up a tail. And he knows it. How long he's been aware of it, I don't know, but say it was before he dropped you off. He's dropped you at your office because he doesn't want to deal with you anymore, because he has more pressing matters on his hands.

"Hitman Number 2.

"Who is Hitman Number 2? Hitman Number 2 is a mob enforcer sent to find out why Hitman Number 1 has not completed his job. Hitman Number 1 is nice enough to leave you out of it, which is why he ditches you before he deals with Hitman Number 2."

"But he didn't ditch me."

"He meant to. You just didn't cooperate. So, Hitman Number 1 ditches you and goes home. On the way, he notices that he's failed to ditch you, but there's nothing he can do about that now. Why? Because he doesn't want to alert Hitman Number 2 to your presence, which he will have to do in order to tell you to stay ditched. See what I mean?"

"In a way. But how does that explain what happened?"

"Okay," Alice said. "Hitman Number 1 goes home, and didn't you say he waited at the desk for Hitman Number 2?"

"That's right."

"Hitman Number 2 arrives and they go up in the elevator together. Creating in your mind the illusion that Hitman Number 2 is the one who lives there."

"You're saying he did that deliberately?"

"Of course he did that deliberately. Look what happens next. After your phone call, I mean." Alice rolled her eyes. "Rollo Tomassi. Hitman Number 1 comes downstairs, confronts you, sends you home, and hops in a cab."

"To convince me the other guy lived there."

"Right. Which works beautifully. Or would have worked beautifully if he hadn't gotten killed."

"So," I said, "Hitman Number 1 offers his buddy a drink, says, 'Oh, I'm out of such-and-such,' runs out, ditches me, hops in a cab, takes it around the block to the liquor store, purchases a fifth of whatever, and goes back to his apartment just in time to get shot."

"He wasn't shot then."

"No, he was shot the next day. By someone who got by the doorman without being seen. And your theory is Hitman Number 2 killed Hitman Number 1 because Hitman Number 1 didn't kill the schoolteacher?"

"That's right."

"So it *is* my fault."

Alice had one of those I'm-going-to-brain-you-with-a-Crock-Pot looks. "Fault? That's probably the stupidest assessment of the situation imaginable. You didn't get anyone killed. At the very worst, you changed the murder victim from a schoolteacher to a hitman. If you actually did anything at all, which I doubt. Regardless, someone was always going to get killed."

That seemed way too pat an explanation. And, if I'd come up with it, I'm sure Alice could have shredded it in seconds. Hearing Alice produce it, I was buffaloed. My chance of talking my way out of this corner was zero.

"In any event, you agree with the assessment that the schoolteacher was the target and the hitman was killed for not taking him out?"

"I think even the police are sold on that explanation."

"The police believe the hitman was trying to whack the schoolteacher?"

"That's right."

"So they put him under police guard?"

"I don't think he's in protective custody. But he's certainly being watched."

"Bad news for Hitman Number 2. The contract's still out on this guy. If he can't deliver, he's in the position of Hitman Number 1."

"He's in very deep shit," I agreed.

"Basically, he's got to kill this guy, or else?"

"That's right."

"So how's he gonna do it?"

29

I HAD ONE ADVANTAGE OVER the police. I'd seen Hitman #2 in person. They'd seen a grainy, overhead, black-and-white profile from a surveillance camera, not much better than the doorman's description. Or mine, for that matter. Mine was terrible in terms of physical characteristics. But I knew the face. I could see it in my dreams.

If I were Crowley, I'd have kept me on the schoolteacher, to see if Hitman #2 came near him. But I'm not Crowley. And Crowley didn't like me, or trust me, or count on my cooperation. He went with plan B, which I discovered the next morning when I went to check out Martin Kessler.

I had no idea when he left for school. Classes started at eight fifteen, but when teachers had to be there was another matter. And I'd never forgive myself if the guy got killed because I wanted an extra half hour's sleep. But, as Alice pointed out, there were so many things I'd never forgive myself for, I could start a Complexes R Us.

Anyhow, I got there at the crack of dawn, figuring no self-respecting English teacher would get up that early. Not to mention any self-respecting hitman. Sure enough, the street outside Kessler's was deserted.

On the plus side, there was a parking spot right down the block, so I could pull into the curb, cut the engine, and have an uninterrupted view of his front steps. Except every time a large truck rolled by. Which wasn't all that often. Not that I expected to miss him in the split second it took for that to happen. Except for the asshole in the fruit truck who acted like he didn't have room to get down the street. *Come on, schmuck. No one's double-parked. That van's sticking out a little bit, but I could drive a 747 through.*

Of course, an uninterrupted view of Kessler's front door wasn't going to do me any good. I didn't have to spot the target. I had to spot the shooter. Where the hell would he be? I had no idea, but I kept turning in the seat, looking in all directions. It wasn't long before I had an incredibly stiff neck. I also realized I was making a wonderful target in the event Hitman #2 spotted me.

About a quarter to eight it all fell apart.

An unmarked police car drove up and Sergeant Thurman got out.

By rights I should like Sergeant Thurman. He's the one police officer who actually makes me look good. A square-jawed, barrel-chested man, Thurman resembles an assistant football coach—big enough to get the job, not bright enough to do it. I have had run-ins with Thurman in the past. He didn't think much of my abilities, and the feeling was mutual.

If Thurman was Kessler's bodyguard, the schoolteacher was good as dead.

Thurman went up the front steps, rang the doorbell, and was buzzed in. I didn't like that. It meant any schnook with the balls to ring the bell and say "Officer Gotsagoo" could get in.

Ten minutes later Sergeant Thurman came out, looked up and

down the street for assassins. He could not have been more obvious had he used binoculars. Satisfied, he went back in and came out with Martin Kessler.

That was an ominous portent. Thurman hadn't spotted me. What were his odds of his spotting a sniper?

Kessler got in the car without getting shot. Sergeant Thurman walked around the front, climbed into the driver's seat next to him. The car pulled out.

So far, so good. Anyone who wanted to kill Kessler would have to kill Thurman. Which would be some consolation.

We got to school without incident. Unless you count getting stuck behind a garbage truck on one of the side streets. I thought Thurman was going to hop out and ticket the guy.

We hit the school at ten after eight. Thurman pulled up at the curb, got out, and looked around. Which was kind of funny. He was in a sea of students. In this mass of humanity, what could he be looking for? What could possibly stand out?

All right, I set myself up for that one. I'm a sexist pig who should have an apple shoved in his mouth and be roasted on a spit. What could possibly stand out but the perky, young breasts of my favorite teacher, bar none, the one I'd met a mere fleeting second when she'd advised me Martin Kessler was still in school. Actually, she'd advised the kids I asked, and not really spoken to me at all, but I think that's being overly technical, considering the extent of the pulchritude.

At any rate, she was in the crowd, and if Sergeant Thurman missed her, he was not only a bad cop, he had probably been neutered.

Thurman, satisfied, bewildered, or just not giving a shit, concluded his surveillance.

I shook my head. Thurman was doing everything wrong. You don't stand next to the protectee. You go in front of the protectee. Look for people taking an interest in the protectee. Thurman's tactic would only work if he had a partner who was hanging back, looking to see if anyone was taking an interest in the two of them. But Thurman always worked alone. Which was not surprising. Who would want to work with Thurman?

Ironically, I would.

I slid from my car, tagged along behind, functioning as Thurman's backup, on guard for any undue interest in Martin Kessler.

There was none, except for Perky Breasts, who pushed through the crowd to engulf him in what had to be one hell of a hug. Evidently, news of his near demise had gotten around, and his fellow colleague wanted to show her support. (Write your own punch line there. I'm in enough trouble as it is.)

Kessler didn't look sorry to see her. But Thurman looked ready to take her down with a flying tackle. Which wouldn't have been that bad a move, all things considered. But his impulse was no doubt based on the assumption the woman was attempting to squeeze the teacher to death. Anyway, he said a few words that caused the young lady to cease and desist, and the three of them marched in the front door.

Ten minutes later Thurman came out, got in his car, and drove off. Which told the story. The police assumed Kessler was safe in school. They'd leave him alone until after classes.

That worked for me. I was tired, and I could use a break.

Before I even had a chance to enjoy the anticipation, Wendy/Janet beeped me with an emergency photo assignment.

30

JEROME ROBINSON, WHO'D FALLEN ON uneven pavement crossing Ocean Avenue, had managed to break his leg, his pelvis, and his neck. I kid you not. At first glance, Jerome Robinson had to be the unluckiest motherfucker who ever lived, sustaining multiple horrendous injuries, each more gruesome than the last. When I interviewed him in the hospital, the poor guy could barely sign the retainer. But sign he did, even if I had to guide the pen. This was one client who wasn't getting away. Richard had gotten a hard-on at the extent of the injuries, and in the event that there was liability, he wanted to be the personal injury attorney with a shot at it.

Which is where Jerome Robinson went from being the unluckiest son of a bitch who ever walked the planet to the luckiest, bar none, because the faulty pavement that tripped him turned out to have been registered. Under New York City's pothole law, only irregularities in the street that had been reported but not repaired made the city negligent. This law, enacted to unclog the court system and keep the city from going bankrupt, was one of Richard Rosenberg's pet peeves. Without it, Richard maintained, he would be wealthy. The fact that he was wealthy in spite of it did not seem to cheer him.

At any rate, nothing made Richard's day so much as a registered pothole. A registered pothole resulting in a broken neck was like winning the lottery. Richard couldn't wait to see the pictures.

Location of Accident pictures are usually taken at the time of the sign-up, particularly when they're in the vicinity and the client is able to point them out. In this case, the sign-up occurred in the hospital, and the client couldn't point at his dick. When that happens, the sign-up is handed in, then Location of Accident pictures will be ordered as a separate assignment if the lawyer decides to take the case.

Due to the extent of the injuries, Richard had told Wendy/Janet to order the pictures at once and dispatch a paralegal to determine the status of the pothole. The paralegal reported back before I got to the pictures. Richard had a shit fit, and Wendy/Janet wore out the phone beeping me to go take them.

Jerome Robinson opened the door to let me in. He was miraculously mobile for a man with a broken neck. Richard would be unhappy with his progress. I wondered if I should send him back to bed.

Mr. Robinson was an agile black man who could have played power forward for the New York Knicks if it weren't for his injuries. Considering the current state of the Knicks, he probably could have played *with* his injuries. He was eager, affable, positively delighted the lawyer was taking his case. I didn't tell him the feeling was mutual. I pointed out how lucky he was to have found an attorney who was thorough enough to have investigated his complaint and found it to have merit. We all agreed on that, and then I went out to take the Location of Accident pictures.

That part of the assignment I could have done for myself. In fact, the entire photo assignment didn't need Jerome Robinson at all. But the gentleman had been so enthusiastic I had been told to call on him to keep him happy. For my money, there was no need. Jerome Robinson was born happy. Even a broken neck couldn't slow him down.

It slowed me down, however. Jerome lived in a fourth-floor walk-up. Game though he might be, an invalid on crutches doesn't go down stairs very well. It would be just my luck to have him fall, break something else, and sue me.

Somehow we made it down and negotiated the two blocks to the scene of the accident.

I had no problem recognizing the pothole. The description and location were right on the money. It was an ugly sucker, an irregular rhombus carved in the street, with jagged bits of tar and asphalt sticking out to lacerate an injudicious pedestrian. It occurred to me it was a good thing I had Mr. Robinson, after all. I could pose him next to it. Show the extent of the defect, nicely balancing the extent of the injury.

"Wow, that's something," I said.

"Tol' you," Jerome Robinson said. "Din' I tell you?"

I turned to him, and the smile froze on my face.

Jerome Robinson was looking in the opposite direction. At a pothole on the other side of the street. A formidable defect, but not nearly as bad as this one. It was round, the edges were smooth, nothing was cracked or jagged. It would be hell to photograph. Only the best lighting and angles could show there was any depression whatsoever. I'd have to stick a ruler in, and even that wouldn't play, shooting from above. It could read as anywhere from half a foot to an inch.

But that was nothing. A mere hiccup. I've taken worse Location of Accident photos before. That wasn't the problem.

It was the wrong fucking pothole. It wasn't registered. No matter how severe the injuries one might have sustained tripping on it, it wasn't worth a cent.

I cleared my throat. "Mr. Robinson, I'm not sure that's your pothole."

He frowned, a 'scuse-me smile on his face. "Wha' you talkin' about?"

"It's important that we're very accurate here. Because we're going to go into court and everything, and they're going to ask you a lot of questions. So we want to be on the same page. Now, you've been laid up in bed for a while. And I've been going on the descriptions and everything. And it seems to me from the story I heard that the pothole that tripped you is most likely this one over here."

Jerome looked, grinned a puzzled grin. "Well, it ain't."

I considered that. Said, "But it might be."

No smile now. "What the hell you talkin' about?"

I put up my hands in a placating manner. "Don't get concerned. I am looking out for your best interests. We all want to get you what you deserve, that's the most important thing. If you think that's the pothole that tripped you, that's good enough for me. Let's go take pictures of it."

We did. From every conceivable angle. With Jerome Robinson beside the pothole grinning and pointing it out. With Jerome Robinson's foot in the pothole to show the size of it. With Jerome Robinson's crutch in the pothole. Hell, I'd have shot one with Jerome Robinson's dick in the pothole if it would have made the guy happy.

When I was done, I popped the roll of film out of the camera, put a fresh roll in.

"Now then," I said, "let's take some pictures just for insurance."

He looked at me. "Wha' you mean?"

I pointed. "The pothole over here. The one you don't think is your pothole. Let's take pictures of it anyway. Tell you why. You've had a hard fall, multiple injuries, including a broken neck. The defense may claim you hit your head, you can't be clear on what

144

you saw, on what you remember. They may introduce an EMS team that recalls picking you up from the other side of the street. Now, we may want to have you testify that you were absolutely clear on where you were hit, and what the other side of the street was. Our attorney may want to put you on the stand, have you point at these pictures, and say, 'That's not where I fell.' Or he may have another use for 'em. I'm not an attorney. But I always know in a situation like this it pays to take as many photos as possible. To keep all your options open and not close any doors. You don't want to hamstring your attorney by doing a half-ass job. So I want to take some pictures of you next to this pothole just to be safe."

Jerome Robinson nodded. "You want me pointin' goin', 'Huh-uh, tha' ain' it'?"

"I don't think so. That would look stagy. I want the pictures to be more from the point of view of you showing the disgraceful condition of the street. Can you do that?"

Jerome frowned. "'Suppose."

And he did. And I shot him. And I didn't feel good about it. Because I was faced with a moral dilemma. And I had failed to take the high ground. I had, instead, taken the coward's way out.

Here was a seriously injured man who needed help. Of all the goldbrickers I'd signed up in my day, the worthless deadbeats with next to no injury hoping to beat the system for a couple of bucks, Jerome Robinson wasn't one of them. He was a seriously injured man who needed help. Help with his medical bills, help from missing work. A man who couldn't afford Aflac and didn't have a duck helping him recuperate. Here he was, dorked by a technicality.

Maybe so, but the law is the law. Circumventing the law is illegal. Attorneys do it all the time. But that, apparently, is their job. And it isn't mine. My job is to gather the evidence and present it to the attorney.

In this case, the evidence indicated the client had fallen in an unregistered pothole, thereby making him ineligible to sue. My job was to gather that evidence and present it to Richard Rosen-berg. The fact that there was a perfectly good registered pothole not fifty feet away was none of my business. If I hadn't known about it, I never would have looked at it. But knowing it was there put me on the horns of a moral dilemma. Should I pursue a suit I knew to be fraudulent? Or should I take the client at his word and photograph his worthless pothole?

Had I done that, Richard would have killed me.

So I had taken the coward's way out. I had passed the moral dilemma along. Here, Richard. Here's the worthless pothole your client fell in. And here's the pothole worth millions that had nothing to do with anything.

Your move.

31

BY THE TIME I DID two more cases and stopped by my office to pick up the mail, all bills, it was close to three thirty when I got back to the school. Thurman's car was double-parked out front. I lucked into a parking space, mingled with the crowd of students hanging out on the sidewalk who either had no last period or were cutting it. I saw a few teacher types, including one who looked almost as much like a football coach as Sergeant Thurman. The teacher of my dreams was not among them. Nor were the baggy-panted presumed dope-dealer and his girlfriend, who didn't figure to be there since they were in Kessler's class.

I wove my way through the students, most of whom were smoking. It was hard to believe kids still did that in the face of the medical evidence now available. They probably figured by the time they grew up there'd be a cure for cancer. That's what my generation figured.

I hung out with the kids, tried to recall what Hitman #2 looked like. On the plus side, he wasn't a kid. That knocked out most of the people present. On the minus side, his features were rather nondescript. Not too old, not too young, not too tall, not too short, not too fat, not too thin. Hair short, dark, and curly; eyes I couldn't begin to tell you; general impression dull, your ordinary everyday working stiff.

Of course, at the time I'd seen him, I'd thought he was the mark. Even knowing he was the shooter, I couldn't build up much enthusiasm for him. As far as I could tell, the guy projected zero personality. Probably a plus for a hitman. He could blend right into a crowd.

But not this crowd. In this crowd of students he'd stand out.

Like I was.

I noticed a certain percentage of the students edging away from me. Which was kind of amusing. I was like a dope-sniffing dog. Drop me into the middle of a group of people and arrest the ones who left.

Anyway, from my vantage point in the center of everything I surveyed the street for signs of drivers. There were some, of course, parents waiting to pick up their kids. None looked like a hitman. At least, none looked like Hitman #2.

I checked the windows in the buildings across the street. All were brownstones. None would offer easy access. But a hitman could pick a lock on a vacant apartment, set up at home while the occupant was away at work. Load his rifle. Adjust his telescopic sight.

I watch way too many movies.

Naturally, I spotted nothing. I didn't figure to. The killer wouldn't show himself so soon. The killer wouldn't make a move until the bell, when school ended and half a zillion kids came out. Then the shooter could slip into the crowd, elbow his way up behind Martin Kessler, and put two rounds in the back of his head before anyone knew what was happening. With an ugly long silencer that barely made a pop.

It could easily happen with Thurman in charge, the good sergeant not even realizing a move had been made on Kessler until the teacher dropped at his feet. Embarrassing though that might be for the police department, it would be totally frustrating for me, the culmination of my utter failure to do my job, losing both my client and the man he'd hired me to protect.

The bell rang, the doors burst open, and a steady stream of students and teachers poured from the building. Mingling into the stream were Martin Kessler and Sergeant Thurman, the latter in full dumbass mode, walking just a step behind, ever vigilant to protect the professor from students who sought extensions on their papers. Jesus Christ, is the guy even looking around?

I was, and I saw her. Just over Kessler's left shoulder. Trailing along as if she were a groupie and he were a rock star. Thurman must not have let her walk with him. An interesting choice, for Thurman. I'd have thought he'd have used her for a shield.

I saw him before Thurman did. To be fair, I'd seen him before and I recognized him. But even so. He was what Thurman was on guard for. Also, to be fair, I didn't see him slip into the crowd. But I saw him making his way through it. Coming up on Kessler from the right and slightly behind. Which also put him on Sergeant Thurman's right and slightly behind. And slightly behind the teacher with the tits. Sorry, but I don't know her name. But he's behind her, and he's got something in his hand. Something gleaming that I can't quite see.

He was in direct line now. Him, her, Kessler, me. With Thurman in front of them and to the left. Thurman hasn't spotted me, I know, because he'd have reacted, most likely to the extent of leaving Kessler entirely forgotten while he reamed me out. But no chance of that. The guy was oblivious.

I could see it all in slow motion. The four of them coming at me. Hitman #2 making his move. Stepping in front of Attractive Teacher. Raising his arm. Just as I stepped in front of Thurman. Heading for Martin Kessler.

It had not been a conscious decision. Trust me, it was not the type of conscious decision I make. Given time to consider it, I would opt for the opposite. But my muscles, as if of their own accord, were sending me forward diagonally across Sergeant Thurman's vision in a long, awkward lunge at Martin Kessler. Tackling the startled schoolteacher and pulling him out of the path of the intended bullet.

Even Sergeant Thurman couldn't miss that. His head turned, his eyes widened in amazement, as Kessler went down. Revealing, directly behind us, Hitman #2, in all his naked glory, silenced automatic raised, aiming at empty air where Kessler had just been, even as he squeezed the trigger.

The bullet whizzed past Thurman's head. Hitman #2 hadn't been shooting at Thurman, he'd been shooting at Kessler, would have killed him if I hadn't knocked him out of the way. That's how close it was.

Sergeant Thurman pulled his service revolver, dropped to one knee, and shot Hitman #2 dead.

32

IT WAS HARD TO TAKE. Sergeant Thurman was a hero, saving Martin Kessler's life by calmly shooting an armed assassin. I was a meddling private eye who'd nearly gotten Martin Kessler killed. Sergeant Thurman was lionized in the press and interviewed on the evening news. I was mercifully not mentioned. At least by the press.

Detective Crowley was not so kind. "Your name is Stanley Hastings?"

"Yes."

"You are aware this conversation is being recorded?"

"I assumed the stenographer was here for some reason."

"You have already been charged with the crime of obstruction of justice. You are aware that anything you say may be taken down and used against you in a court of law with regard to that charge or any other that might arise in the course of the interview?"

"That's a mouthful."

"Are you aware of the gravity of the situation?"

"Yes, I am."

"Are you aware of your rights as I just explained them?"

"I'm aware of the *situation* as you just explained it. I don't believe any rights were mentioned."

"You have the right to an attorney. Do you wish to have an attorney present for this interview?"

"No, I don't."

"You are waiving your right to an attorney?"

"It's Richard's poker night. I try not to call him on his poker night. He gets grouchy."

"What were you doing today at Harmon High?"

"I'm a fan of Sergeant Thurman. I like to watch him work."

Crowley scowled. "This is no laughing matter."

"Neither is Sergeant Thurman."

"Mr. Hastings, did you observe the shooting this afternoon at Harmon High?"

"Yes, I did."

"Can you tell us what happened in your own words?"

"I've never understood that expression. Who else's words would I be using?"

"You're taking this awfully lightly."

Yes, I was, and I'm not sure why. Maybe it was having a bullet whistle over my head. Maybe it was seeing someone shot dead in front of me.

But I think it was the horrifying realization that in a moment of crisis I had instinctively acted bravely in the face of danger, had exposed myself to harm rather than covered my head. It was clearly a moment of weakness, immediately suppressed, never to happen again, but it left me giddy with a light-headed sense of foolhardiness such as I had never experienced before, with the possible exception of the time I lost my mind years ago in Atlantic City when everyone was trying to kill me. The situation was hardly parallel. The danger here had been sudden, instant, and brought on by myself. Nonetheless, I was still riding the high.

"Sorry," I said. "What's the question again?"

"Just tell us what happened at Harmon High."

"Around four fifteen I saw Sergeant Thurman and Martin Kessler come out the front door."

"What were you doing there?"

"Watching Sergeant Thurman and Martin Kessler come out the door."

Crowley scowled. "*Why* were you there?"

"To see if anyone took an interest in Martin Kessler."

"Are you on the police force?"

"You know I'm not."

"Yes, I do. I wondered if *you* were aware of it."

"I'm not sure your sarcasm will show in the transcript." I looked at the stenographer. "Is there any way to indicate the detective is being facetious?"

"Why don't you leave us to sort out the transcript and confine yourself to answering the questions?" Crowley said.

I shrugged. "Whatever floats your boat." I swear, I'm usually cooperative. It was just one of those things.

"Can you please tell us what you saw and did with regard to Martin Kessler at Harmon High?"

"Kessler came out the front door of the school. Sergeant Thurman was with him." I saw no reason to mention any other teachers, no matter how perky-breasted they might be. "A man approached Kessler with a gun. I pushed Martin Kessler down. Sergeant Thurman shot the man dead."

"You didn't trip and fall?"

"Is that what Thurman says?"

"It's not true?"

"Yeah. I fell down. On broken pavement. I may sue the City of New York."

"The man who was shot—had you ever seen that man before?"

"Yes, I had."

"When was that?"

"In the lobby of Victor Marsden's apartment building."

"Was that man your client?"

"Who? Victor Marsden?"

"No. The man *with* Victor Marsden. The man who was shot dead this afternoon. Was he your client?"

"I'm afraid I can't answer that question."

"Why not?"

"If I do, you're going to ask me another."

"That's not legal grounds."

"What about my right to remain silent?"

"You gave up the right to remain silent."

"Now I want it back again."

"You can't remain *selectively* silent. You either talk or you don't."

"All right, I don't."

"You already talked."

"Yes, and now I'm done. Unless you'd like to try another topic." I cocked my head. "How about them Mets?"

I can't be sure, but I think the stenographer had a narrow escape from a giggle.

Crowley flipped his notebook open, checked a page. "You know a man named Frankie Delgado?"

"Who?"

"Frankie Delgado. Do you know him?"

"I don't know."

Crowley frowned. "What do you mean, you don't know? You either know him or you don't."

"People don't always give their right name."

"Have you met *anyone* who gave the name Frankie Delgado?"

I nodded approvingly. "Good work, detective. Most people would be put off by that evasion, think it meant I might have known the man under a different name. You realized what I said could also mean that he *gave* me the name Frankie Delgado, but I had no way of knowing if it was true."

"I'm not sure I realized all that," Crowley said, "but I certainly would like an answer."

"What's the question?"

"Do you know a man named Frankie Delgado?"

"Who's Frankie Delgado?"

"Frankie Delgado was the man shot dead this afternoon in front of Harmon High."

"How did you get his name?"

"He was carrying a wallet."

"Be careful of jumping at conclusions, detective. It's easy to get phony IDs."

"Are you suggesting his name *isn't* Frankie Delgado? What name did he give you?"

"He didn't give me a name."

"No?"

"No. My parents did. Stanley. After a great-uncle on my mother's side." I snuck a look at Crowley, to see if he might be weighing the consequences of punching a subject under interrogation in the presence of a stenographer.

He ignored my remark. "Did your client tell you his name was Frankie Delgado?"

I was about to make another wiseass answer when it dawned on me that Detective Crowley wasn't as pissed off as he ought to be. It didn't take a genius to know why. I'd told him I was done talking. He'd trotted out the name Frankie Delgado to goad me into speech. He was happy to have me clown around. Maybe I'd slip and actually say something.

"Where'd you hear the name Frankie Delgado?" Crowley persisted.

I suppressed the impulse to tell Crowley I'd heard it from him, then shut the hell up before I hung myself from my cocky little jockstrap.

33

THIS TIME ALICE WAS SCARED. "My god, you could have been killed!"

"I'm fine."

"Yeah, this time. What about next time?"

"There won't be a next time."

"Stanley, I know you. You have an addictive personality."

"No, I don't."

"Oh? What about your lattes and scones?"

She had me there. I practically live in the Silver Moon Bakery, which has to be the best thing that ever happened to our neighborhood. I have a cranberry scone every morning and a raisin bran muffin for lunch. The fact Alice does, too, in no way deters her from kidding me about it.

"You did something dangerous. And you got away with it. It doesn't mean you'll get away with it again."

"I know."

"You're all keyed up and you think you're Superman."

"I don't think I'm Superman."

"You knocked a guy down."

"I knocked a guy down."

"And saved his life."

I waggled my hand. "Awww."

"See?" Alice said. "You throw modest in with it, it's a recipe for disaster. Here you are, an elderly—"

"Elderly?"

"Middle-aged geezer acting like a comic book hero. Of course it's going to go to your head."

"Nothing's going to my head."

"No kidding."

The TV came back from commercial. Alice snapped it off mute.

The heading read: SHOOTOUT ON THE UPPER WEST SIDE.

"An armed man was shot dead at a public high school after firing his weapon at a police officer. Sergeant Thurman of the NYPD had been assigned to a schoolteacher believed to be in danger. It was a good thing he was."

The news cut to a close-up of Thurman with a microphone shoved in his face by an on-camera reporter. "We came out the front door of Harmon High and I observed the perpetrator aiming a weapon at the protectee."

"What happened then?"

"A civilian panicked and tripped. I was lucky he didn't knock me over."

"What did you do?"

"Pulled my gun and shot the perpetrator."

"Shot him dead?"

"That's right."

"Why was it necessary to use such deadly force?"

"He discharged his gun. As soon as he fired, I fired. Luckily, my aim is better."

Alice muted the volume again. "Did you trip?"

"No, I did not."

"I'd like it better if you tripped."

"I'm sure you would."

"Don't go getting brave on me. I don't need you getting brave on me."

"Never fear."

"See? You even sound cocky saying that. Look, I don't mean to be a wet blanket. You shouldn't get bawled out for saving the guy's life. But it's scary, Stanley. I don't want anything to happen to you."

"Nothing's going to happen to me. Look, the police weren't taking this seriously before. They'll take it seriously now."

"What do you mean, take it seriously? They had an officer on him."

"Yeah, Sergeant Thurman."

"He did his job."

"He did his job because I coughed and said, 'Excuse me, Sergeant, but there's a man with a gun over here.'"

"You mean you tripped?"

"Yeah, right. Anyway, I think we can count on the police to keep Martin Kessler on ice for a while. Not to mention that Sergeant Thurman bumped off Hitman Number 2."

"That's right. He did."

"So what are you afraid of?"

Alice shrugged.

"Hitman Number 3."

34

RICHARD WAS OFFENDED. "You didn't call me."

"You were playing poker."

"I'd have come."

"I didn't want to bother you."

"Bother me?"

"Particularly after last time."

"That was a stray bullet. This is a little different. Someone was shot dead."

"But it wasn't a murder."

"What?"

"It was, and I think Sergeant Thurman will bear me out on this, self-defense. The hitman fired first. I don't think there's any way you could call it a murder."

"I don't care if you call it a barn dance, you should have called."

"You were very specific. Not just any gunshot. Call you if it's a murder. I have to admit it was borderline. But, seeing as how I was a witness and all, I'd have to tip the scales in Sergeant Thurman's direction."

"So Thurman killed the hitman?"

"That he did."

"Bang, over, finished."

"From his point of view."

"Thurman's?"

"The hitman's."

"Uh-huh. So, that's taken care of for the time being?"

"Yes, it is."

"Good. Because I was very worried about you. Very worried. You're my best investigator. I depend on you."

"I'm flattered."

"So, with all that going on," Richard said, casually, "did you have time to get out to Ocean Parkway?"

I suppressed a smile. Richard had been dying to ask me about the Location of Accident photos but felt obliged to feign at least a token interest in the shooting first.

I snapped open my briefcase, took out a packet of photos, threw it on Richard's desk.

He picked them up, flipped through them. "Oh, my god! These are fantastic! Fantastic! I was afraid they'd rush out there and fix the street. Not that it would lessen the liability, but then we wouldn't have pictures. You cannot *believe* the difference a good visual can make in a jury's award."

"Sounds like I deserve a bonus."

Richard caught himself in mid-gloat. "Stanley. You know how these things are. All contingency cases. If I win, I get paid. If I lose, I don't. I can work on something for eight months and have it get thrown out of court. You get paid whether I win or not. Hell, you're probably charging me two hours for these simple photos that took you ten minutes to take."

"Three hours, Richard."

"*Three* hours?"

"Travel time, Richard. My last case of the day. Travel time there and back."

"It's only your last case of the day because you were out getting arrested."

"I wasn't arrested."

"Whatever. The point is, you're getting paid, and I might not."

"I'm glad to see you're so broad-minded."

"Huh?"

I reached in my briefcase, threw another packet of photos on Richard's desk.

He frowned, picked it up, pulled out the prints. "What are these?"

I smiled.

"Funny you should ask."

35

MacAullif was on Thurman's side. That figured. Everything else was upside down in this stupid case. Why shouldn't he back a moron?

"I didn't trip," I protested.

"You didn't stay on your feet, either."

"I really don't want to argue, MacAullif."

"Who's arguing? I'm not arguing. I'm just pointing out if Thurman says you were on the ground, it's because you were on the ground."

"So I was on the ground. There are many ways of getting there. He's a sergeant. You're a sergeant. I rest my case."

"Let me be sure I got this straight. Are you saying you tried to save the guy?"

"I know that's hard to believe."

"Oh, I can imagine you *trying*. You *succeeding* is something else."

"You forget I was saved by Sergeant Thurman."

"I don't see why you're busting his balls. He could have let the hitman shoot you."

"Delgado wasn't trying to shoot me."

"I don't see why not. You're an insufferable pain in the ass. There's times I'd like to shoot you myself."

"Come on, MacAullif. Frankie Delgado was our only lead. So numbnuts shoots him dead."

"I admit he will be harder to interrogate."

"How am I going to find out why he killed my client?"

"Ah, that's more like it. Totally at sea, with no idea how to do your job. That sounds more like you. Tell me, are you mad at Thurman because you can't question Frankie Delgado, or are you mad at Thurman because he did your job. To put it another way, would you be feeling right about this if *you* shot Frankie Delgado?"

"I haven't got a gun."

"Exactly. So you feel inadequate. So you're pissed off at the guy who has."

"Jesus Christ, MacAullif. Are you in therapy?"

"No. Why?"

"I'm just wondering where you come up with this amateur analysis."

"Gimme a break. It's just common sense. The gun is an extension of your penis. If you don't have one, you got no dick. You're like a neutered dog resenting one with balls."

"Thanks a lot."

"That's for your therapy crack. But there's something to it. If you were armed, you wouldn't feel powerless."

"If my witness were *alive*, I wouldn't feel powerless."

"Your witness wasn't going to *talk*. Your witness was going to *kill people*."

"Yeah, well, maybe he had a bad childhood."

"Yeah. Maybe he couldn't get laid in high school and had a small dick. Anyway, this time around you're not going to get much mileage portraying Sergeant Thurman as the villain in the piece. He's a hero cop, plain and simple, probably get a citation."

"I know."

"And you think it isn't fair?"

"Do you?"

"Who gives a shit? Maybe it isn't fair, but your problem is you think it should be fair. You think there should be a giant scale somewhere, and all the good deeds and bad deeds get weighed, and then everyone gets what they deserve."

"Are you sure you're a cop?"

"Why?"

"The images you come up with."

"Okay, you think it's like a TV show, where by the end the bad cop gets his comeuppance and the good cop saves the day."

"Are you saying Thurman's a bad cop?"

"I'm not sayin' shit. I'm tying to deal with your dumbass notions."

"Thanks a lot. So what do I do now?"

"Jesus Christ, it always comes down to this. Here you are, in my office, asking what to do next. Here's what you do next: nothing. It's got nothing to do with you anymore."

"What about Kessler?"

"What about him? He's still alive, thanks to Sergeant Thurman. He's in protective custody, thanks to this asshole Thurman shot. He's not going to school anymore. He's bein' babysat by the cops."

"For how long?"

"Until we find out who's pissed at him."

"With Thurman in charge? That could be a long time."

"Thurman's not in charge."

"Oh? Who is?"

MacAullif raised his eyebrows.

"You!?"

"No, not me, asshole. What have I got to do with it? Detective Crowley's in charge."

"You're kidding."

"Hey, it's a homicide."

"No, it's not. It's self-defense.

"Not this bozo. What's-his-face. Victor Marsden."

"They got the guy who did it. Didn't the bullets from Delgado's gun match up?"

"That's what I hear."

"So, isn't the case solved?"

"In an unsatisfactory way."

"Thank you. You mean Sergeant Thurman *isn't* the cat's meow?"

"Sergeant Thurman is Sergeant Thurman. You take the good with the bad."

"Easy for you to say. He never messed up your case."

"Well, I wouldn't go that far."

"Really? What'd he do to you?"

"He didn't *do* anything. He's made mistakes, sure, but he's always meant well."

"He should get points for that?"

"Well, with all these movies about bad cops. Actors just love to play 'em. The dirtier the better. Didn't Denzel Washington win an Oscar for one? There's something to say for a cop who's honest."

"He's a saint. So what do I do now?"

MacAullif grimaced. "That's the third time you've asked me. Jesus Christ, you're like one of those fucking writers doesn't know where to go with his story, just sits spinning his wheels. What do they call that?"

"Writer's block."

"Yeah. That's it."

"And do you know how to solve that, MacAullif? 'Cause there's a lot of writers gonna be pretty damn grateful."

"I don't know what they do. But I know what you do."

"What's that?"

"See what happens next."

36

I WENT OUT ON MY rounds. I didn't know what else to do, and I needed the money. Not that I really expected Richard to charge me umpty million dollars for keeping me out of jail. Keeping me out of jail was one of Richard's hobbies. A nice break from the usual negligence shit. Of course, I realized I shouldn't abuse it. As Richard had pointed out. If you ask me, he was just being cranky. Obstruction of justice is a serious enough charge. Especially when it's regarding a murder. Surely Richard could get his rocks off with that and not bill me up the wazoo.

Anyway, Rodney Walks, in what passed for a house in Bed-Stuy, Brooklyn, had developed lead poisoning from eating peeling paint. Probably not the smartest move, but Rodney was only two years old and not up on the latest surgeon general's warnings. His mother, however, did know better, and was righteously indignant. Oddly enough, largely at Rodney himself.

"I tol' him not to eat the paint, and he jus' keeps eatin' it. Jus' don' listen. Got no sense."

I figured that was probably true. Rodney, a toddler, would be prone to poor career choices and not quick to take direction. I wondered why the mother, who clearly did know better, hadn't realized the Socratic method wasn't working and taken the initiative to remove the paint from the child or the child from the paint. But, hey, it wasn't my problem. I took down the woman's information, didn't comment on her parenting skills.

She was signing the retainer when my beeper went off. I called in, and it turned out I was wanted in the office.

"At the end of the day?"

"No, now," Wendy/Janet said. "Finish your sign-up and come in."

I signed up the paint eater, who'd probably make a small fortune from his horrific diet. Had the mother known that? Was she actually a very bright woman who sat in the corner *feeding* him chips of poison paint?

I beat it back to Manhattan, lucked into a parking meter, took the elevator up to the offices of Rosenberg and Stone.

Wendy was on the desk. I can tell 'em apart in person. She was on the phone, but she waved me in.

Richard was at his desk writing on a pad. At least that's how it would look to a client. I knew him well enough to know he was doodling.

"What's up, Richard?"

He smiled. "Sit down."

Uh-oh.

I pulled up a chair, waited for the bomb to drop. "What's the trouble?"

"What makes you think anything's the trouble?"

"You're being entirely too nice."

"I resent that."

"Okay, what's up?"

"The Jerome Robinson case."

"Why am I not surprised?"

"I had a nice talk with the client. Smart man. Reasonable. But concerned."

"Why is he concerned?"

"The photo assignment. When he pointed out his pothole."

"What about it?"

"Jerome feels he may have been mistaken."

"Does he now?"

"Yes, he does. And he's rather upset about it."

"I'm sorry to hear it. He seemed a nice man."

"He is a nice man. And he's suffered a terrible injury."

"He's making a miraculous recovery."

Richard frowned. "Yes. What's *that* all about? Anyway, the gentleman now feels that the pothole that tripped him was the jagged one that was registered but not repaired."

"So what's the problem?"

"He's afraid your memory may not agree with that opinion."

"No, that's the one I thought it was, too," I said innocently.

Richard scowled irritably. "Yes, but he *didn't* think it was at first."

"He seemed prone to make that mistake," I agreed.

"But now he'd like to correct it."

"What's the problem?"

"He's afraid you'll contradict him. He's afraid you'll take the stand and say he's lying."

"*Is* he lying?"

"Of course he's not lying!" Richard controlled himself, smiled ingratiatingly. "He made an honest mistake."

"Then he has nothing to worry about."

"That's what I told him. But he's not convinced."

"What do you want from me?"

Richard smiled, his most ingratiating smile. "Could you talk to him? Reassure him? He's at the point where he could go either way. He needs someone to talk him down."

"I think you switched metaphors on me."

"Can you do this for me?"

"On top of what I already did for you? Taking the pictures of the pothole the client said had nothing to do with his accident?

The one on which you're basing your entire case now? The one you gloated would be enough to up the jury award, though not to the point I should get any bonus out of it. So I can pay all your billable hours for keeping me out of jail."

"Consider it done. I was joking, Stanley. I'm not going to charge you."

"I know you were joking, Richard. So not charging me isn't a concession on your part, is it?" I interlaced my fingers, twiddled my thumbs. "It seems that the merits of the cases that you take are rather flexible. Now, this one, for instance, if you go by the pothole the guy claimed, has absolutely no merit whatsoever. On the other hand, if you consider the registered pothole, it's a whole different story."

"You've made your point. What do you want?"

"Medical malpractice, the same thing. From one point of view, a woman with a dead baby isn't worth anything. From another point of view, maybe there's something to be done."

Richard's eyes widened. "Son of a bitch!"

"Do we have a deal?"

"I can't believe you're doing this."

I couldn't believe I was, either. But my life was upside down, and something had to make sense. Or work out. Or seem fair. Somehow, in the cosmic order of the intergalactic mind-fuck, I needed something to go my way. Yolanda Smith and her dead baby was just the ticket.

"Do we have a deal or not?"

"Of course, we have a deal."

"Good. Catch you later."

I got up to go.

"Stop by the front desk and see if Wendy or Janet have any new sign-ups." Richard didn't care if I did, he just wanted to reassert his authority.

I wish I could have let him. "Not this afternoon, Richard."

He blinked. "Oh? Why not?"

"I'm going to a funeral."

37

I GUESS I WAS EXPECTING the Sopranos.

No one at Victor Marsden's funeral looked the least connected. Just a bunch of ordinary, everyday people, marking the impact of death upon their lives.

And it didn't take place in a huge cathedral, with half a dozen pallbearers loading a massive coffin into a hearse followed to the cemetery by a parade of stretch limousines. No, the Victor Marsden funeral was a quiet little affair at the Johnston Funeral Home on Third Avenue, where a pneumatic elevator whooshed you up to the fourth floor and spit you out into a thickly carpeted room just large enough for the dead man and his guests.

The coffin was closed, probably a wise choice for a gentleman who'd been shot in the head. Anyway, Victor was presumably in the box, which looked to be somewhere between pine and mahogany, not your dollar ninety-nine egg crate, but not your plush-lined Stratosleeper with gold-embossed lid and built-in stereophonic eternity tape. No, it was as plain as could be.

So was the woman dressed in black and seated off to the left, the one the guests approached to pay their respects. She was clearly Victor's mother, which disconcerted me. Hitmen didn't have mothers. Except Tony Soprano, and she died after the first season. Yet here, in all her white-knuckled grief, sat Mrs. Marsden, clinging to the arms of the chair as if holding on to her son, pulling him back from that awful place, keeping him safe, while mourner after mourner knelt by her and reaffirmed the fact that he was not.

The gathering was so sparse that I stood out. Not that anyone cared. Not that anyone was paying the least bit of attention. Clearly, no one knew that much about their dear departed friend. Nor did they know each other. People were talking in small groups of two or three. There weren't more than twenty people there at all.

Which made me rather conspicuous. At least I felt conspicuous, just standing there with no one to talk to. Which was good, because I wouldn't know what to say. But I could feel Mom's eyes on me, trying to figure out who I was. Which, I realized, was just in my head. The woman couldn't possibly have cared. Still, it occurred to me someone else might notice that I was just hanging out, that I didn't belong. Which was totally ridiculous. How would they know?

I looked at Mom.

She was looking back.

I went up to her, knelt down, said, "I'm sorry. He was a good man. I'll miss him."

She looked at my face, probably wanted to ask me who I was. But didn't want to be embarrassed if I turned out to be someone she should know. She just smiled a thin smile, said, "Yes, he *was* a good man, wasn't he?"

"Yes, he was," I said. "I'm very sorry."

And I stood and moved on.

I could sense the woman's relief. She didn't have to go through an awkward conversation, conceal the fact she couldn't place me when I told her I went to Swarthmore, or wherever the hell her son went. Anyway, I was happy not to compound the woman's grief.

The next obstacle was the guest book, stationed between the mother and the coffin. One couldn't really avoid it after paying one's respects. It would be crass not to sign my name. It would also call attention to me. So I had to sign.

My real name? Should I sign my real name? Leave a record of the fact I'd attended this funeral? For the cops to find?

I could imagine Detective Crowley's blood pressure going through the roof when he read the register and found my name. But why would he? Was that the sort of thing Crowley would do? It was the sort of thing MacAullif would do, if it were his case. Talk about going through the roof!

I could sign John Doe. Or John Hancock. Or Jack Armstrong, All-American Boy. I might as well sign my own name, a hollow subterfuge like that.

Good Christ, I gotta sign something. I can't just stand here. Signing my name shouldn't be this hard.

Fuck it.

I signed *Stanley Hastings.*

If that freaked anybody out, it was too damn bad.

Now what?

The minister. Or reverend. Or priest. Or whatever the hell they called themselves. Was this Catholic? It didn't look Catholic. Damn. That's what happens when an atheist marries a nonpracticing Jew. Not that Alice needs practice.

My god, I'm flipping out. Who is he, and do I need to talk to him?

I suddenly remembered I had to go to the bathroom. That is to say, I *pretended* I had to go to the bathroom. Which sounds strange. I didn't start wobbling my knees and grabbing my crotch. I just mean I glanced around the room as if looking for the bathroom. And I'm an actor. A method actor. What's my motivation? Stanislavsky. I'm sure *he* went to the bathroom.

Anyway, in my head I was avoiding an uncomfortable and potentially dangerous conversation with the minister by looking for the men's room door. An Oscar-caliber performance. *I'd like to thank the Academy* . . .

Just about then it occurred to me that attending the funeral of Victor Marsden had accomplished absolutely nothing.

And in walked my favorite perky-breasted teacher.

38

SHE LOOKED GOOD IN BLACK. A new trend. Grieving chic.

She didn't notice me. Though why should she? She breezed right up to the mourning mother, knelt down beside her. Hugged her, exchanged a few words. Then moved on, signed the guest book. Right under my name. Which meant nothing to her. Unless she didn't read it. Why should she? Why shouldn't she?

She spoke to the minister. He wasn't that old. His face lit up when he talked to her. She had that effect on men. Even men of the cloth.

I wondered if she knew anyone there. She finished with the reverend, looked around, gave no sign of recognition, and anyone would have recognized her.

I wandered by the guest book, stole a casual glance.

The perky-breasted teacher was Sheila Blaine.

I sidled up to her, said, "Hi."

She looked at me as if I were trying to pick her up. Which, in a way, I was.

She smiled, said "Hi," but her body language said "Do I know you?"

"You'll excuse me if I'm forward, but I don't know anybody here."

"I don't either."

"You know the mother."

"I met the mother. I don't really know her."

"Let me take a wild stab. Ex-boyfriend?"

"Why do you say that?"

"Funerals aren't much fun. Not the type of thing you'd go to for a casual acquaintance."

"Who are you?"

"I ask myself that every day. Sorry. Scratch that. You saw me at the school. I'm the one who pushed Martin Kessler out of the way. Before he got shot at."

"Oh. You're the man who tripped."

"Amazing how that story stood up."

"Story?"

"So you're Victor's ex. Do you know what he did for a living?"

"He was in the stock market."

"Is that what he told you?"

"That's what he did."

"Dangerous work, the stock market."

Her eyes narrowed. "What are you saying?"

"I've known a few stockbrokers. This is the first one I've heard of shot dead."

"It's not funny."

"I wasn't joking."

"What *were* you doing? What are you trying to say?"

"You're also friends with Martin Kessler."

"He's a fellow teacher."

"He's a *married* fellow teacher."

"You have a dirty mind."

She was right. I did. But I wasn't the one messing around with a married fellow teacher. I wondered if I should point that out to her.

It occurred to me that if I were quicker on my feet, I'd have already come back with a retort rather than wondering whether I ought to.

"I didn't see you interviewed on TV?"

"No. Just Marty and the hero cop."

"Marty?"

"He's a colleague. You want me to call him Mr. Kessler?"

I wasn't making much headway with the young woman, except she hadn't told me to go to hell. I wondered why not.

"What were you doing there?" she asked.

"What do you mean?"

"Before you tripped."

I winced. "You trying to goad me?"

"I was joking before." She peered at my face. "But you're really pissed about it, aren't you?"

I smiled. "No. It's fine if you think I fell down."

"What were you doing there?"

"That's the wrong question."

She frowned. "What do you mean?"

"You should be asking me what I'm doing *here*."

"What *are* you doing here?"

"Paying my respects to the dead."

She pouted. "You're the one who said to ask you."

"Your two gentlemen friends—did they know each other?"

"Please! Martin Kessler isn't my gentleman friend."

"But Victor Marsden was."

"I said he was an ex-boyfriend."

"You go to the funerals of all your ex-boyfriends?"

"No. Only those who die."

"That's an interesting answer. I can't decide if it's cold and callous, or spunky."

"Maybe I don't care what you think."

I nodded. "There's absolutely no reason why you should. I wonder if it's occurred to you yet."

"What?"

"So far, you're the only connection between Victor Marsden and Martin Kessler. In a twenty-four hour period, someone tried to kill 'em both."

"What about you?"

"What *about* me?"

"*You* knew both of them."

"Yeah. As far as I know, we're the only two people here who can make that statement."

"Are you a cop?"

I grimaced. "I get that in the projects a lot. I hoped for something better from you."

"So who are you?"

"Stanley Hastings. I'm a private investigator."

From her expression I had just shattered her illusions. She thought a PI was Jack Nicholson in *Chinatown*. Only she was probably too young for that.

"Oh," she said. "I'm—"

"Sheila Blaine," I said smoothly. "Pleased to meet you."

"How do you know my name?"

I jerked my thumb. "You wrote it in the book."

She frowned. Disappointed.

"Yeah," I said. "Tricks aren't much fun when you know how they do them."

She adjusted her parameters, said, "Are you here on the job?"

"No."

"How about at the school? Were you on the job then?"

"No."

"I don't understand."

"I don't either. But I'm trying to."

"Why?"

I sighed. "Lady, I wish I knew."

39

I TOOK HER TO A small coffee shop on Lexington, bought her an iced latte, tried to calm her down.

It wasn't easy.

"Why?" she said. "Why would anyone do this?"

"You know what Victor did for a living?"

"I told you. He was in the stock market."

"Yeah," I said dryly. "Very cutthroat business."

"Are you mocking me?"

"Sorry. Were you aware Victor had a sideline?"

She grimaced. "That's what I hear. Ties to the mob. I can't believe it."

"How long were you involved with him?"

"Two years."

"You get to know a person pretty well in two years."

"I thought I had."

"And now?"

"I don't know what to think."

"That's a little different from, 'I can't believe it. Victor wouldn't do such a thing.'"

"He wouldn't."

"And yet you don't know what to believe."

Her eyes flashed. "No, I don't. You wanna make something of it? I went with the guy for two years. I thought I knew him. Suddenly he's shot, and I start hearing reasons why. You wouldn't be upset? You wouldn't be confused? You wouldn't wonder what to believe?"

"Did he ever give you any indication he had another life?"

"No." She bit her lip. "There were times. A dinner or a show, canceled on short notice. I remember calling around seeing if anyone wanted to go to *Spamalot*."

"What excuse did he give?"

"He had business."

"Stock market business?"

"You're saying I was stupid?"

"You were in love. Credulous."

"I wasn't in love," she protested.

I wondered if that was true. Or merely an opinion formed since the breakup.

"What about Martin Kessler?"

"What about him?"

"What's he to you?"

"A colleague."

"Good word! In one way. Bad in another."

"What do you mean?"

"You had it ready. In case you were asked. Which means you *expected* to be asked. Now, why would that be?"

"Sometimes I have lunch with Marty. People talk."

"Did Victor know about Marty?"

"No! I mean, there's nothing *to* know. Marty is just a friend."

"Victor ever see you at lunch with Marty? Maybe stop by your table casually? You say people talk? Could Victor have gotten the wrong impression?"

She frowned. "What are you saying? Victor saw me with Marty, got jealous and attacked him, and Marty killed him in self-defense? Is that what you think?"

I sighed. "I don't know what I think."

"Because that is just about the stupidest thing imaginable. I mean, look at Marty, look at Victor. You think Marty takes him? Come on!"

"With a gun?"

"Give me a break! Marty never fired a gun in his life. Even if he did, it would never happen."

"If he was cornered . . ."

"Victor wasn't like that." She took a sip of her latte. "I remember one party he thought I was flirting with another guy. He didn't say a word. Not to him. *I* got an earful. Victor could be very sarcastic. But to the guy he just smiled and nodded. Nice as could be. Next time I see this guy he's having all kinds of trouble. His car wouldn't start. His credit card got cancelled. And Domino's delivered twenty pizzas to his apartment."

"And you think it was Victor?"

"Of course it was Victor. Real practical joker. It didn't bother him the guy never knew. *He* knew. Son of a bitch."

"So, if he knew about you and Marty . . ."

"There's nothing *to* know about me and Marty."

"But if he *thought* there was . . ."

"He might have sent him a pizza. Believe me, it wouldn't have gotten him killed."

I was sure it wouldn't have.

I was learning nothing of importance from the perky young schoolteacher, and it occurred to me I wasn't apt to. I had been seduced, not by the woman but by the coincidence of her knowing both my client and the man my client was supposed to kill. Only that's all it appeared to be. Coincidence. She hadn't known them at the same time. If she were telling the truth, she was, at best, an unlikely source of information. In light of which, my taking her out for coffee had served no useful purpose, except to bathe in her perkiness.

Alice was going to have a field day.

40

"YOU PICKED UP A GIRL?" Alice was at her taunting best. Eyebrows raised, teasing smile.

"I didn't pick up a girl."

"I thought you said you went out for drinks."

"Yes."

"From a funeral."

"Yes."

"Isn't there a scene like that in *Wedding Crashers*?"

"Alice."

"How cute. You actually picked up a girl. At your age. I'm impressed."

She was also impressive. Alice was lounging on the bed in a T-shirt that always reminds me of Mary Louise Parker in the *West Wing* episode where she dances in Josh's kitchen. I saw the episode again, and the T-shirt Mary Louise Parker is wearing doesn't look anything like it. Go figure. This does not diminish the allure, however. When Alice wears the T-shirt, she tends to distract me from my appointed task.

"It was business," I protested.

"Oh? Were you on the job?"

"That's what *she* said."

"Huh?"

I explained my conversation about my involvement in the case.

"So, you took her to a bar."

"A coffee shop."

"A coffee bar?"

"If you want to call it that."

"What did you have."

"We had iced lattes."

"We?"

"Okay. *She* had an iced latte. *I* had an iced latte."

"You're being very defensive."

"I'm being nothing of the sort. I'm trying to answer your questions, and you don't like the answers."

"Well, I'm trying to adjust. It's not every day you pick up a girl in a bar."

"I picked up a girl at a funeral."

"And you took her to the coffee bar to . . . ?"

"Turn her inside out and see what makes her tick."

"Oh. Lofty goal. I think. How did she look inside out?"

"Alice."

"So what did she tell you?"

"Not very much."

"It was a complete waste of latte?"

"I got some information."

"Such as?"

"She'd been with Marsden two years. Met him at an art show."

"An *art* show?"

"I don't make the facts, I just report them."

"And what was the young lady doing at an art show?"

"Looking at art."

"And meeting men."

"I don't know if that's why she went. She did happen to meet one."

"And she stayed with him for two years and then he got shot."

"She stayed with him for two years, then she *left* him, and then he got shot."

"Right away?"

"No. There were some intervening months."

"During which time she took up with the teacher?"

"She denies it."

"Of course, she denies it. He's married."

"You doubt her word?"

"Of course."

"You don't even know her."

"I see her through your eyes. It's like watching a movie. And you took her to a coffee bar where she denied having an affair with the married schoolteacher. How long did that take?"

"Not long."

"You cross-examined her on it. Really pinned her down. But she had no problem, since she was telling the truth."

"Is that irony? Are you being ironic with me?"

"Of course not. That would be catty. You're not accusing me of being catty, are you?'

"Certainly not."

"So what's her connection with the dead man? Aside from the fact he's her ex-boyfriend? How ex is ex?"

"She said six months."

"Had she seen him lately?"

"Oh."

"That didn't seem like a good question?"

"It wasn't what I was interested in."

"I'll bet."

"I think you're missing the big picture here."

"What big picture?"

"The dead man said he was supposed to kill somebody and told me he was Martin Kessler. Then *he* got killed, and his name wasn't Martin Kessler. Then somebody tried to kill Martin Kessler. What's wrong with this picture?"

"Nothing," Alice said. "It's just like I told you. The victim was always Martin Kessler. That's why he gave you that name. But he didn't want to kill Martin Kessler, so someone killed him. Then that someone tried to kill Martin Kessler."

"Say that's true. Then how do you explain the girl?"

"What's to explain?"

"Are you kidding? It's a monumental coincidence. They both know the same girl."

"But it's *not* a coincidence." Alice looked at me as if I were a moron. "Don't you get it? *She's* the key. The guy's been going about his merry business, bumping off people right and left. Until now. What happened? Someone asked him to kill his ex-girl-friend's current boyfriend. That is more than he can handle. He goes out of his way to avoid having to do it."

I blinked. "Can it be that simple?"

"Why not?"

"Well, you're talking about a hitman with a heart of gold. He wants to spare the guy who took his girl? Are you kidding me? Most men would want to kill the guy who took his girl."

"Maybe," Alice said. "But you're talking about a hitman with a heart of gold anyway, the minute he wants to spare anyone. Hitmen blow your brains out, get paid, and that's that. They don't give it a second thought."

"Yeah, but . . ."

"But what?"

"It's a far cry from having scruples to being a saint. You gotta assume the guy knew who Kessler was the minute he heard the name. He could have just said, 'I'm personally involved, pass it on to someone else.'"

"Who?"

"I don't know. Whoever killed *him,* for instance."

Alice wasn't convinced. "So, what did you tell her your involvement was in all this?"

"I told her I was a friend of Victor Marsden. I want to find out why he was killed. Strictly on my own. I told her my investigation wasn't professional."

"There's an understatement."

"Alice."

"Did she buy that?"

"I don't know."

"Couldn't you tell?"

"No, I couldn't. I feel like I'm juggling so many balls in the air I don't know which is which."

"And what was the reason for your interest in Martin Kessler? I mean, how much did you tell this girl?"

"If *I* were calling her a girl you'd be all over me. In a manner of speaking."

"You wanna answer the question?"

"I was vague and evasive."

"That's hard to believe."

"Where did you get that T-shirt?"

"Don't change the subject. We're not talking about me, we're talking about her."

"You're more attractive."

"Now you're just pissing me off. How old is this girl?"

"Old enough to be called a woman."

"Old enough to vote?"

"Alice."

"So, you told her you're a PI, swept her off her feet."

"I didn't sweep her off her feet."

"Did you tell her you're a PI?"

"No fair. I already told you that."

"So, you told her you're a PI." Alice shook her head, pityingly. "No wonder the poor girl fell so hard."

"Alice, the girl couldn't care less about me."

"Oh, now she's a girl?" Alice rolled her eyes. "Stanley, you're about as perceptive as the average tree slug. Particularly when it comes to women. Trust me, she's smitten. She probably sees you as a father figure, but nonetheless. I'd watch out, if I were you."

I grinned. "Oh, really? And just why is that?"

"Numbskull!" Alice spread her arms, reasoning with an idiot. "Someone tried to shoot her last two boyfriends."

41

MacAullif wasn't much better. "You went to the guy's funeral and picked up a witness?"

"Someone had to."

"What do you mean by that?"

"Crowley wasn't interested in her."

"How do you know?"

"He didn't even question her."

"Sure he did."

"Huh?"

"You're talking about the schoolteacher with the pointy breasts? He questioned her right after he questioned you."

"Then how come she wasn't on TV?"

"You weren't on TV."

"I know, but . . ."

"But what?"

"She never mentioned being questioned."

"Did you ask her?"

"Not specifically."

MacAullif shook his head. "And you wonder why you make no progress." He took a file off his desk, flipped it open. "Would that be one Sheila Blaine?"

"I think so."

"You *think* so?"

"Yeah, that's her name."

"Crowley questioned her."

"About the shooting at the school?"

"Yeah."

"But not the Marsden shooting?"

"No."

"And you ridicule *my* interrogation techniques."

"Nothing connected her to the Victor Marsden shooting. She was questioned as an eyewitness. Nothing else."

"So Crowley missed the connection."

"Crowley didn't go to the funeral."

"It would have been a good move, as things worked out."

"Yeah," MacAullif said. "You know how much free time I'd have if I went to the funeral of every homicide victim I was investigating? I'd never see a movie again. Or have a backyard barbecue. I'd be divorced in a year. Should I go on?"

"Is Sergeant Thurman still on the case?"

"He's on paid leave, pending review. Routine for a fatal shooting."

"When's he get his medal?"

"You're really pissed, aren't you?"

"Even Perky Breasts thinks I fell."

"It's not in her statement."

I picked up the file. "You have her statement?"

"Oh, you got it bad, haven't you? I take it this is one comely teacher."

"You haven't seen her?"

"When would I see her?"

"You said the teacher with the pointy breasts."

"Just goin' on what I hear."

"Wait a minute. A simple eyewitness is important enough cops are talking about her?"

"No. A simple eyewitness has perky enough tits people are talking about her. Jesus Christ, get your priorities straight."

"Okay," I said, changing the subject. "If Thurman's not protecting the schoolteacher, who is?"

"By that I assume you mean the one who got shot at? Not the one you're infatuated with."

"Come on, MacAullif. Who's on the case?"

"Everybody and his brother. Guy can't take a piss without someone recording the fact."

"Is he going to school?"

"Not so you could notice."

"What's the point? If the police have him sewn up, no one's gonna make a move on him."

"That's what they're hoping."

"So the case is never solved and the guy spends the rest of his life in protective custody."

"What makes you think the case will never be solved?"

"Well, is anyone tracking down leads? Someone tried to kill this guy for a reason. How about finding who he's involved with who might care whether he lives or dies?"

MacAullif smacked himself on the forehead. "Oh, my god! What a great idea! Thank goodness you came down here today. I'll pass that suggestion right along."

"So they've already done that. Okay, what did they find?"

"Nothing. The guy's clean as a whistle. Doesn't drink, smoke, gamble, or take drugs. Doesn't owe a bundle to any loan shark. Bought his apartment ten years ago for eight hundred and twenty thousand. Price is for the midtown location. The apartment's not that big. Been paying the mortgage on it ever since. Mortgage is paid up. Blue Cross Blue Shield. He's got life insurance."

"How much?"

"He's worth two million dead. Four million if it's accidental."

"What about the wife?"

"What about her? Lovely lady. Wife and mother. Homemaker. But . . ."

"There's a but?"

"Drug bust in college. Cocaine. Paid a fine, did community service."

"Cocaine?"

"Yeah."

"You need a lot of money to do that."

"That you do. And if the little lady was still tootin', she might have done the shootin'."

"She was standing right next to me when it happened."

"I mean the hiring. It just didn't rhyme."

"I don't like it, MacAullif."

"I hate it like hell, but the facts are the facts."

"Come on. How does a woman like that find a mob hitman?"

"How did the perky schoolteacher find one? It's not a physical impossibility, you know."

"The schoolteacher never hired a hitman to kill anyone."

"How do you know?"

"What?"

MacAullif shook his head. "Your problem is you believe everything people tell you. What if she wasn't the guy's girlfriend at all? What if she hired him to kill Kessler?"

"Why would she do that?"

"How the hell should I know? Maybe he's a clingy son of a bitch she can't get rid of. You know the type. Won't accept the fact it's over. Cramps her style in terms of meeting anyone else."

"So she kills him?"

"These are not gems, just suggestions. A lot of them are going to be wrong."

"Can you connect Mrs. Kessler to the hitman?"

"Which hitman?"

"*Any* hitman. Victor Marsden. Frankie Delgado. Bruce Fucking Willis in *The Whole Nine Yards*. Amanda Peet."

"Who?"

"His girlfriend. In the movie. She was a hitman trainee."

"Oh."

"Is the woman dirty?" I persisted.

"Amanda Peet?"

"Mrs. Kessler!" I glared at MacAullif. His eyes were twinkling. "You did that on purpose. Can't you tell I'm drowning here."

"I don't see why. You're not a cop. You really have no obligation to solve this case."

"Except I'm charged with obstruction of justice."

"Yeah," MacAullif admitted grudgingly. "I bet that charge would go away if you butt out and let the cops do their job."

My eyes widened. "Was that a bribe? Did you just offer me a bribe?"

"Certainly not."

"Or a threat?"

"A threat?"

"The implied inverse. If I *don't* butt out, they'll prosecute me to the full extent of the law."

"That's not the case at all. Though it's an awfully good suggestion."

I sighed. "Okay. What about the other end?"

"What other end?"

"Marsden."

"I ran Marsden for you, remember? Contract killer with ties to Tony Fusilli. Strictly small-time."

"That was when he was alive and kicking. Now he's dead, he's more important. You say he worked for Tony Fusilli."

"So?"

"And Frankie Delgado?"

"Same thing."

"Just what is Tony Fusilli involved in that would require the services of a hitman? More to the point, what is Tony Fusilli involved in that might shorten the life of a Manhattan school-teacher?"

"Sounds simple, doesn't it?"

"Simple and obvious. I don't know why you haven't already done it."

"Well, for one thing, it's not my case. But if it were, what could I do? Investigating Tony Fusilli is no walk in the park."

"The cops are scared of him? You ask him questions, wind up dead?"

"That's not the point. You don't just walk up to Tony Fusilli. Tony Fusilli has lawyers, and layers and layers of protection. You wanna find out something about Tony Fusilli, you do it discreetly on the sly."

MacAullif took out a cigar, drummed it on his desk. "That's for starters. Then you factor in the diversity of the man's holdings. Tony Fusilli has real estate. Tony Fusilli has trucking. Tony Fusilli has import/export of everything from olive oil to automobiles. And that's his legitimate business. Then there's all the fucking stuff he shouldn't be doing. Do you know how many people are lining up to talk about that?"

"You don't have to dig into all that. You just have to find a logical connection to Martin Kessler."

MacAullif stuck the cigar in his mouth as if he were going to smoke it. He wasn't, of course. His doctor had made him quit. But he waggled it at a jaunty angle.

"Be my guest."

42

TONY FUSILLI LIVED IN A fortress. A thirty-three-story building on Tenth Avenue in the garment district. Tony owned the whole thing. His penthouse triplex was rumored to be nice. Not that anyone had ever seen it. The majority of Tony's work force never made it past the thirtieth floor.

I didn't even make it past the lobby.

"Who?" demanded a uniformed security guard/doorman who looked like he could have played tackle for the New York Giants. At one time he probably did.

"I want to see Tony Fusilli."

"Is he expecting you?"

That was one of those questions you answer it wrong, you're out on your ear. It was a close call, but I figured the wrong answer was yes. He'd check, discover the lie, and tie me into a few perfect sailor's knots. "No" didn't seem promising either, but it had the advantage of being the truth.

I gave it a try.

"Then he won't see you," the guard said promptly.

"But he wants to see me," I said. "At least he will when he knows I'm here. How would I tell him I'm here?"

"You would call him on the phone."

"That phone?" I said, pointing to the one on the security desk.

"Sure."

I picked up the phone, said, "What's the number?"

"You don't have the number?"

"No."

"How you gonna call if you don't have the number?"

"I'll buzz upstairs. How do you buzz upstairs?"

"I punch in the number."

"What number?"

"Mr. Fusilli's number. You don't have it?"

"No."

"Too bad."

I hung up the phone, said, "Who *can* I talk to?"

"Me."

I took a breath. "No disrespect meant, but we're kind of talked out. Who else could I talk to?"

"You want to talk to someone else?"

"Yes."

"Who?"

"One of Tony Fusilli's officers."

"Which one?"

"The one you have the number for."

"I have all their numbers."

"Okay. I want to talk to whoever has Tony Fusilli's ear."

He shook his head. "Sorry. I have to have a name."

"I haven't got a name."

"Or a number."

"Extension 23."

He nodded approvingly. "Nice try. I'm sure some phone systems work that way."

The guy was a son of a bitch. It occurred to me if this were a book, I'd come back in a later chapter and give him his comeuppance. In real life, I'd probably never see him again.

While we were arguing, Tony Fusilli came in. I'd never seen Tony Fusilli, but I knew it was him because he was wearing a pinstripe suit that cost more than your average three-bedroom condominium, and more jewelry than a fortune-teller, rap star, and sultan combined. I also knew because he came with an entourage of henchmen whose total IQ probably didn't pass a hundred, but who obviously were heavily armed, plus two geniuses by comparison—a tall man in a three-piece suit and a pudgy, curly-haired man in a rumpled jacket and tie—most likely his lawyer and his accountant.

I also deduced it from the fact the security guard snapped to attention and said, "Good afternoon, Mr. Fusilli."

The bejeweled Donald Trump wannabe turned a cold eye on me and said, "Who's this?"

I couldn't ask for a better cue. "Mr. Fusilli, I need to see you. It's rather urgent."

Cold eyes burned into me. "Was I talking to you?" To the security guard he repeated, "Who's he?"

"He wanted to see Mr. Fusilli, but he says you're not expecting him."

"Then why is he still here?"

That wiped the smile off the security guard's face. I grinned at his discomfort.

"I was just getting his story before sending him along."

Fusilli smirked. "Oh, big shot. As if you could actually do that. Instead of just impressing him with how important you are." He jerked a finger at the tall lawyer-looking type in the three-piece suit. "Joey, stay down here, find out what the guy wants."

Joey nodded, started for me.

The pudgy, curly-haired man in the rumpled jacket put out his hand and stopped him. "Joey, I need you upstairs with me. Louie, you do it."

The rude, aggressive son of a bitch I'd taken for the big boss said, "Yes, Mr. Fusilli," and the hierarchy fell into place. The pudgy, curly-haired man in the rumpled suit was Tony Fusilli. I had pegged everyone wrong. It was almost reassuring.

Tony and the entourage went upstairs, which left me with faux-Fusilli and the security guard.

"Tony doesn't have his own elevator?" I observed.

"He does," the security guard said. "But it goes straight to the thirtieth floor."

"Motor-mouth!" Louie said. He took me by the shoulders, led me out of earshot. "What do you want with Mr. Fusilli?"

"I want to save him some trouble."

He scowled. "Get specific, douchebag, and I do mean now."

"Martin Kessler."

He was poker-faced. I'd have thought the name meant nothing. If I didn't know better.

"What about him?" he demanded.

"You know who he is?"

"No."

"That's strange. How about Victor Marsden?"

I think his eyes flicked on that one. Though I couldn't swear to it.

"Who's that?" he said.

I shook my head. "Not good. Kessler you say, 'What about him?' then deny you know him. Marsden you say, 'Who's he?' to head off the question of whether you know him."

"You talk funny. Are you a cop?"

"No."

"I didn't think so. Let's see some ID."

I took out my investigator's license. "I'm Stanley Hastings. I want to talk to Tony Fusilli."

He looked at my ID and laughed. "Oh. Private. You must think you're hot shit."

I said nothing, flipped my ID closed, slipped it back in my pocket.

He scowled. "What's your business with Fusilli?"

"The cops can tie him to a couple of murders. I thought he'd like to know."

"Oh, sure. If the cops could tie him to a murder, they'd be here. You know it, they know it, I know it. Anything else is bull-shit. Like what you're bringing me."

"You don't wanna know what I know?"

"You don't know dick. You're on a fishing expedition. You're in here pretending you know something, hoping to get someone to talk."

For a moron, he was right on the button. I was on a fishing expedition, which was hard to deny since I *didn't* know dick.

"I know Marsden worked for Fusilli. I know Frankie Delgado did, too. The cops know it, but they're chicken-shit to act. I thought Tony might like to know how I know."

The "Tony" was pushing it. We didn't really have a personal relationship, and this goon knew it. Still, when you're bluffing with nothing, you might as well go all in.

He wasn't buying it. "You aren't seeing Mr. Fusilli. Anything you want to say, you say to me."

"Martin Kessler is under police guard. You can't get to him. Whatever he knows he's gonna tell. You can keep trying to take him out if you like, but, frankly, you're just wasting button men."

"I don't know what you're talking about."

"I think you do. And I think Tony Fusilli's gonna be real upset when he finds out you didn't let me warn him. I would imagine he is not a good man to have angry at you."

If Louie was scared, he didn't show it. Except by acting even more belligerent, which could have been a sign of nervousness. Or could have been a sign of belligerence.

"Get the fuck out of here!" he snarled.

I did.

43

I PICKED UP A CRANBERRY currant scone and an iced latte from the Silver Moon Bakery and went home for lunch.

My wife was crouching. Crouching wife, hidden agenda.

"I've been thinking about the schoolteacher," Alice said, nibbling on my scone.

That caught me up short. I was two dead hitmen, one funeral, and a meeting with a mobster removed from thinking about Martin Kessler. Not to mention, when Alice said schoolteacher, my first thought was Miss Perky Breasts. In light of which, I was perfectly happy to talk about Martin Kessler.

"What about the schoolteacher?" I said, covering beautifully.

"If the hitman was supposed to be following him—"

"Which hitman?"

"Your hitman. Hitman Number 1. Victor Marsden. He was supposed to be following the schoolteacher, right?"

"Right."

"Did you see him?"

"Who?"

"The schoolteacher. Martin Kessler. When you followed Hitman Number 1, did you see him tailing the schoolteacher?"

"No. I saw him tailing Hitman Number 2. What's-his-name. Frankie Delgado. The guy who killed him."

"Allegedly."

"I don't think we have to protect his reputation. The guy is dead."

"But you saw your client tailing him?"

"That's what I *thought* I saw. Now it appears what I actually spotted was Hitman Number 2 tailing *him*."

"Did you see him after they dropped you at your office?"

"Who?"

"Hitman Number 2."

I shook my head. "Not till he showed up at Marsden's apartment. But then I wouldn't have."

"Why not?"

"I was tailing Marsden."

"You were always tailing Marsden."

"Yeah, but he didn't know it. I mean then. Before, Marsden knew I was tailing him. It was part of the job. After he left me at the office, I figured I was done, he didn't want me anymore. So I was tailing him without his knowledge."

Alice snorted. "As if."

"Okay, okay. The point is, I didn't spot Hitman Number 2 because I was keeping far enough in the background so Marsden wouldn't spot me." I raised my finger. "And, Hitman Number 2 didn't spot me."

"How do you know?"

"If he had, he would have told Marsden."

"What if he did?"

I frowned. "What do you mean?"

"Maybe that's why Marsden came down and shooed you away.

Because Hitman Number 2 told him you were there. So he would have come down and chased you away even without the brilliant phone call."

"Yeah, but . . ."

"But what?"

"Hitman Number #2 doesn't know me. How can he spot me? I'm just any other guy."

"Who'd been following Marsden all day. He spots you following him from your office. He spots you following him *back* to your office. He spots you after you're presumably *left* at your office. It doesn't take a genius to figure out, wow, this guy's everywhere."

I bit my lip.

Alice took a sip of iced latte. "What I can't understand is how you spot this hitman and you can't spot the schoolteacher. If Marsden was following the schoolteacher, you should have seen him."

"I didn't know him."

"Did you know Hitman Number 2?"

"No. But I started seeing him in different places."

"Ah! What a coincidence. The same way Hitman Number 2 spotted you."

"Yeah. So?"

"So, why didn't you spot the schoolteacher? The same way you spotted the hitman? Why didn't you see him in a few places? If Marsden's following him? You may not have known what he looked like, but you know what he looks like now, and you don't recall seeing him, do you?"

"No."

"So why would you miss the amateur and spot the pro?"

"I spotted the pro because Marsden wasn't following him."

Alice frowned. "What?"

"Marsden was trying to keep me from spotting the guy he was following. Being a pro himself, he doesn't have much trouble doing that. On the other hand, Hitman Number 2 is following

202

Marsden, and has no idea Marsden is being followed by anyone else. Hitman Number 2 probably spots the guy Marsden is following. He knows perfectly well who it is. He's following Marsden because Marsden hasn't killed him. Hitman Number 2 is keeping Marsden in sight, keeping the target in sight, and keeping the two of them from seeing him. What he's *not* looking for is someone *else* picking up his back trail."

"All right, all right," Alice said. "Maybe that's why you spot the pro. But why don't you spot the schoolteacher?"

"I have no idea. Unless Marsden wasn't following the schoolteacher."

Alice spread her arms. "There you are."

I blinked. "Alice. It was *your* idea that he was following the schoolteacher."

"No, it wasn't."

"With the bus, and the fish, and the Metrocard transfer. Remember?"

Alice waved it away. "That was how it *could* have happened. I never said it *did*."

My mouth fell open. I was sure she said it did. I just couldn't prove it. I wished, for the thousandth time, I had a microcassette recording to back me up. "Well, I certainly got that impression."

She patted me on the cheek. "You're very impressionable."

"If Marsden wasn't following the schoolteacher, what was he doing?"

"*Not* following the schoolteacher."

"Huh?"

"He was *supposed* to be following the schoolteacher. But he wasn't. He was playing games with you. That's why he was killed. For *not* following the schoolteacher."

"Isn't that the same as following the schoolteacher and not killing him? In terms of motivation, I mean?"

"What's your point?"

203

I had no idea. As usual, when talking to Alice, I found my brain two or three paragraphs behind. I had a feeling that Alice's theory about the schoolteacher was probably important, if I were only swift enough to pick up on it. But I wasn't, and Alice had once again outdebated me.

She had also finished my scone.

44

I WAS IN QUEENS SHOOTING a wet floor in Wendy's, always an iffy assignment. You either sit there all day waiting for someone to spill something, or you pour it on the floor yourself. Which makes me feel like a real sleaze. Which is stupid, since *any* picture you take is going to be staged. The soda the client slipped in isn't still there, it evaporated, or got licked up by a dog, or the floor was mopped, or whatever. So the photo for a slipped-in-water case doesn't mean shit. The attorneys for the defense will have an easy time arguing that it's inadmissible. But Richard will argue that it shows the layout of the restaurant in question, and the judge will allow it for a limited purpose, and Richard will have won, because, limited purpose or not, the jurors aren't going to ignore the water on the floor.

Anyway, I was contemplating buying a Diet Coke to spill, when Wendy/Janet beeped me to call MacAullif, and he told me to come in.

"Why?" I asked, but he'd already hung up the phone.

So I bagged the dubious photo assignment and headed back to Manhattan.

MacAullif had a cigar out, a very bad sign. In fact, he was already drumming patterns on his desk.

"What's up?" I asked him.

"You recall a talk we had earlier? About Tony Fusilli?"

"I'm not that senile, MacAullif. Get to the point."

"I'm wondering if you made pass at the guy."

"I'm not gay." I held up my hand. "Not that there's anything wrong with that."

"Did you go anywhere near Fusilli, you make a move on Fusilli, you talk to anyone related to Fusilli? I mean in a business sense. Anyone in Fusilli's extended family. Anyone at all."

"You gonna tell me why you're asking?"

A large vein was bulging out in MacAullif's forehead. I couldn't recall having seen it before. "Just once could you answer a fucking question without asking one of your own? I need to know if you're involved with Fusilli. I'd like to get that information before someone else gets it who may not interpret it so kindly."

"Jesus Christ, what the hell happened?"

"Did you go see Tony Fucking Fusilli, yes or no?"

"I saw him."

"Jesus Christ!"

"You broke your cigar."

MacAullif had snapped it in two. He looked from hand to hand, seemed surprised to find it that way. "Unbelievable!"

"You're the one who told me to do it," I protested.

"I did nothing of the sort."

"You said 'Be my guest.' When I asked if I could talk to him, you said 'Be my guest.' "

"I was being sarcastic. Couldn't you tell I was being sarcastic?"

"Must have missed it. Anyway, I went over to Fusilli's place. Not that he'd talk to me."

"Did anyone?"

"Now, that's another question."

MacAullif stood up so hard his chair hit the wall. "I'm trying to cut you a break here. You don't seem to want it."

"That's because I don't know what the fuck you're talking about, MacAullif. You want to stop being so cagey and let me in on the secret."

"I will if you'll answer one more question without asking one of your own."

"Shoot."

"You happen to talk to Louie Russo?"

"Why, is he dead?"

"Jesus Christ! You couldn't do it! One fucking question, and you couldn't fucking do it!"

"Is that a yes?"

"Yes, he's dead. Shot a couple of dozen times by someone who was really mad at the fuck. Now, do you think you could do me the courtesy of assuming I know my job and answer a fucking question?"

"A couple of dozen times?"

"Yeah. Whoever killed Louie was really pissed off. I start thinking what could piss someone off that much, and I think of you."

"I didn't talk to Fusilli."

"No, you talked to the guy who got shot. Which I'm sure is a coincidence."

"You being sarcastic again?"

"Read my face."

"I didn't get the guy killed, MacAullif."

"How do you know?"

"Our conversation was unenlightening."

"I'll be the judge of that."

"You expect me to remember what we said?"

"I'd like the gist."

"Just what you'd expect. I ran a bluff, trying to get information."

"What did you get?"

"Not a damn thing. Guy called me cold, accused me of running a bluff, told me to get lost."

"What did he spill?"

"Not a goddamned thing."

MacAullif shook his head. "That doesn't compute. You talk to the guy, he goes upstairs, someone's so pissed off they shoot him six ways from Sunday. Now what did the guy let slip?"

"Not a thing."

"He must have."

"He didn't."

"All right, if that's what you think, he must have told you something you didn't get. He let something slip that would have meant something to anyone with half a brain."

"Thanks a lot."

"Oblivious Man doesn't get it. But Tony Fusilli, who doesn't realize he's dealing with Oblivious Man, thinks Louie's spilled the beans."

"What beans? The guy didn't tell me anything."

"You just *think* he didn't. You gotta go back over the conversation, see if anything sticks out."

"It doesn't."

"Thank you for your open-minded attitude. That will make this so much easier."

"I can't help it, MacAullif. The guy gave me nothing. I can go over it and over it, and he still gave me nothing."

"All right. What did *you* tell *him*? What did you say that might put his boss in a rage?"

"I didn't say a thing."

"That's how you bluffed him? I can't imagine why it didn't work."

"I told him Kessler was in protective custody and they'd never get to him."

"That's not quite nothing."

"That's not quite news, either. He's been in it since yesterday."

"Nonetheless, it illustrates what you mean by nothing. Now, what other nothings did you tell him?"

"I told him Marsden and Frankie Delgado were dead. I said the cops knew they were Fusilli's button men, they just couldn't prove it."

"This is also nothing?"

"This is nothing that's going to send Fusilli into a rage and make him shoot his own man. Why would he do that?"

"I have no idea, because I don't know the context. Neither do you, but you write it off anyway because you're too lazy to figure it out."

"Come on, MacAullif. I told him the two dead guys worked for him. This is not news to him. Why would it piss him off?"

"I don't know, because I wasn't privy to the conversation."

"Privy?"

"Right. Like an outhouse. Like your mind. Is there anything you're not telling me?"

I thought about it.

"There was another guy there."

45

THE COPS SWEATED THE SECURITY guard for hours. He'd have ratted me out if he'd known who I was, but the guy didn't know my name. I'm sure Crowley would have loved to put us together, but I was nowhere to be found. I wasn't answering my beeper, at least not officially. I was knocking off cases, I just wasn't calling cops.

MacAullif didn't give me up, bless his heart. The minute I mentioned the security guard, he suggested I get out of there. I did, not a moment too soon. I barely got to my car before my beeper started going crazy.

To the cops' credit, they questioned Fusilli and his men, for all the good it did them. As one would expect, Fusilli's henchmen presented a united front. Louie had stopped in the lobby to talk to some troublemaker, and was never seen again. It was suggested that the cops question the troublemaker. Since they couldn't find him, they sweated the security guard instead. That was his comeuppance for being an asshole. I wish I could have seen it. I would have in a book.

As things were, I wanted no part of Detective Crowley. Instead, I wound up in another no-win conversation with my wife.

Alice was waiting at the door when I got home. "Stanley! Are you crazy? You called on a mobster!"

"What, no amenities? No 'Hi, honey, how's your day?' "

"Where have you been?"

"Working."

"It's eight thirty!"

"I worked overtime."

"Why didn't you call?"

"I didn't want to get my messages."

"I'll bet. The police called."

"Just once?"

"No, a lot. I let the answering machine pick up."

"Good girl."

"Bad boy. You called on a mobster?"

"Is that what the cops said?"

"The third or fourth time. You called on a mobster, and now he's dead!"

"I don't think it's cause and effect."

"But you *did?*"

"We got anything to eat?"

"I made chicken."

"Great."

"Two hours ago it was great. Now it's food."

We went in the kitchen and Alice zapped the chicken curry in the microwave while I gave her a rundown of my meeting with Louie Russo.

"I don't get it," Alice said. "You didn't tell *him* anything. He didn't tell *you* anything. And he gets killed."

"That's right."

"So you had nothing to do with it."

"I *must* have had something to do with it."

"Maybe it's just coincidence."

"How can it be coincidence?"

"What, exactly, did you tell him?"

"I told him Hitman Number 1 works for Tony Fusilli. And I told him Hitman Number 2 works for Tony Fusilli."

"That's gotta be important."

"How can that be important."

"Maybe it's important that you knew it."

"He didn't kill *me*. He killed Louie Russo. Why is it important if Louie Russo knows it? He *already* knows it."

"What if he didn't? What if this is the first Louie heard these guys worked for Fusilli? So he goes to Fusilli with that information."

"That makes no sense."

"Why not?"

"*Everybody* knows they worked for Fusilli. The cops know it. The mobsters know it. It's in their record. You check out these guys, it's what you come up with."

"All right, so what else did you tell him?"

"I didn't tell him anything."

"You just think you didn't." Alice opened the microwave, took out the plate of chicken. It smelled delicious. "You want this chicken?"

"Of course I want that chicken."

"Then tell me one other thing you told this mobster."

"Alice!"

"What?"

"You're going to withhold food until I tell you?"

"Why not?"

"That's as bad as withholding sex."

"There's an idea."

"Alice!"

"Come on. Think. What else did you tell him?"

I took a breath, blew it out. "I told him the cops had the schoolteacher and there was no way to stop him from talking."

"I'm not sure that's worth chicken."

"Alice."

"Come on. What else you got?"

"I told him if he didn't let me warn Fusilli, he'd be sorry."

"And he *was*." Alice slid the plate in front of me. "Interesting."

I'm glad Alice thought so. As far as I was concerned, it was utterly irrelevant, boring as hell, and had nothing to do with anything.

But the chicken sure was great.

48

I GOT A LATE START next morning. I stayed asleep, and Alice walked the dog. I usually take Zelda out, but today I didn't even hear her. I guess I was really wiped.

And not from lack of sleep. Just from stress. Just from being on constant guard to defend myself on all sides. I don't mean from physical attack. I'm a New Yorker. I'm generally wary. I mean from getting in too deep. With cops. And mobsters. And lawyers. And clients. And meter maids. And IRS auditors.

You're probably wondering where some of those personnel come in. The tax man and the meter maid, for instance. Well, I live in Manhattan, we have alternate side parking, and I keep the location of my car, and what day and time I have to move it, in my head, or I risk a parking ticket even more expensive than a tank of gas. That's where the IRS agent comes in. Deducting the ticket I can't afford as a business expense and seeing if he buys it.

Anyway, I sprang out of bed at ten after nine with a full twenty minutes before my car, parked on the north side of 104th Street, had to be moved. I showered at the speed of light, climbed into my clothes. I was still tying my shoes when the elevator arrived. I hopped in on one foot, pushed L, finished my laces, and started in on my tie. I had it loosely knotted by the time we hit the lobby. I snatched up my briefcase, and darted for the door, shirt collar up, tie trailing behind me in the breeze.

I came out the door at nine twenty-nine. Sure enough, my Toyota was the only car on the north side of the street. And there on West End Avenue, waiting for the light, about to turn the corner, was not just Lovely Rita, Meter Maid, but Courtesy, Professionalism, and Respect himself, a genuine police officer in a genuine police cruiser, who would be happy to accept my illegally parked car as quota from heaven, a gift from the alternate side parking gods, the very second that nine thirty rolled around.

I sprinted half a block to the car, fishing the keys from my pocket and punching the remote button for the code alarm as I came. Headlights flashed, the locks popped open.

I snuck a look behind me.

The cop hadn't even turned the corner yet.

Hot damn.

I wrenched open the door, flung my briefcase on the seat, hopped in, and started it up.

I couldn't tell if the cop was coming because my mirror was folded in. On the side streets, you always fold the mirror so it won't get sheered off by someone passing a double-parked van. I lowered the passenger side window and leaned across the front seat to push the mirror.

A bee flew by my head. I knew it was a bee because it buzzed, and because I'd just opened the window, which could have let one in. I have to tell you, I don't mind bees outside, but not in a car. A bee in a car has nowhere to go. It keeps bumping into you until it gets pissed off and stings you. And who wants to get stung in the face by a bee?

Anyway, I ducked my head to avoid that happenstance and hit the window button to let the sucker out.

That's when I saw the hole in the windshield.

Bees don't make a hole in the windshield. Or, a bee that does is a bee to be reckoned with. But I didn't think that was the case.

Trembling all over, I peered over the edge of the seat in time to see the cop pull up behind me. I kicked the door open, slid out, and flattened myself against the side of the car.

The cop, who'd just gotten out of his cruiser, was surprised to see me. "Hey, buddy. Can't park here."

"Officer!" I gasped.

"I was just going to give you a ticket. I didn't see you in there."

"Yeah, yeah! Look, you gotta help me!"

"Sure, buddy. First you gotta move your car."

"Shit!"

"Hey! Watch it, buddy!"

"Oh, for Christ's sake! You see the bullet hole in the windshield?"

His eyes narrowed. "You got a gun?"

And there I was, once again, caught in a shaggy dog story with a moron who wouldn't listen.

"No, I don't have a gun, I'm not moving my car, and there's something I want you to do right now!"

"What?"

"Arrest me!"

47

"The bullets don't match."

"Oh?"

Detective Crowley shook his head. "The bullet from the upholstery of your car doesn't match the bullets from the body of Victor Marsden."

"I wouldn't expect it to, since that gun is in police custody. At least I hope it is."

Crowley looked lost for a moment.

"The bullet that killed Marsden is a bullet from the gun on the body of Frankie Delgado, the man Sergeant Thurman killed. That better not be kicking around."

"You're talking very wise for a man in your position."

"Someone who just got shot at?"

"No. I mean a murder suspect. You've been ID'd as the last man to see Louie Russo alive."

"Really? I don't recall being picked out of any lineups."

"You're identified from the picture."

"What picture?"

"Your mug shot. From your booking for obstruction of justice."

"Oh, that's fair. Show your witness a bunch of photos, one of which is a mug shot."

"That's not what we did."

"Were your other photos mug shots?"

"Most likely."

"Most likely?"

"The police supplied the pictures for the identification. I'm sure they were the same."

"There's your reasonable doubt right there. I hope the rest of your investigation's better managed."

Crowley stuck his chin out. He shouldn't have. It made him look more boyish. "You're a wiseass son of a bitch, and from what I hear, you got no reason to be."

"People are shooting at me. It makes me cranky."

"That hasn't been confirmed."

"What? Oh, I'm on the Upper West Side, so you *expect* a stray bullet?"

"You could have fired it yourself."

"What?"

"The cop who found you doesn't recall hearing a shot. Just seeing you pop up out of your car."

I put up my hands. "Wait a minute, wait a minute. I fired a shot through my windshield into my car, ditched the gun, and hid on the floor and waited for a cop to arrive?"

"I admit it sounds unlikely."

"No kidding."

"Except it was nine thirty. Just in time for alternate side parking. The cop was *due* to arrive. If you shot the bullet earlier and ditched the gun, you could go out just before nine thirty, wait till you see a cop coming, and duck down on the floor-boards, knowing he'll stop at your car because at nine thirty you're illegally parked."

I stared at him. "You know, if you'd apply half as much logic to solving the crime, we wouldn't be here."

"Oh, we're working on that too," Crowley said airily. "It's just every time we turn around, you pop up. I thought I told you to butt out."

"I did butt out. I don't care what you think, I didn't shoot at myself."

"No, but you got Louie Russo killed, and you don't even know why."

"I don't even know *if*. You're making a lot of assumptions, Crowley."

"Oh, we can ID you all right. You're the guy who spoke to Louie."

"I mean about the conversation getting him killed."

"Well, what do *you* think got him killed?"

"I have no idea."

"Well, I do. You talk to the guy and he gets killed and you get shot at."

"You're admitting I got shot at?"

"Say you did. Then there was something in that conversation that was dangerous to someone else."

"Well, you're wrong."

"You admit you had the conversation?"

"I'm not admitting anything. But if I *did* have that conversation, there would be nothing in it of harm to anyone."

"How do you know?"

"Because I wouldn't have mentioned anything anyone didn't already know, and neither would he."

"This conversation you're alluding to—the one you're not admitting you had—if you *had* had it, what would you have said?"

"What do you mean?"

"Without admitting you had a conversation, could you recon-
struct as closely as possible what you might have said?"

"You want me to speak hypothetically?"

"Yes. Can you do that?"

"Just don't tell my wife."

48

I TOLD ALICE ANYWAY. MUCH as she hates hypotheticals, this one was different. In the absence of Richard, I had to look out for myself. After all, people were shooting at me.

"Why aren't you in protective custody?" Alice wanted to know.

"You mean like in a hotel room with two police guards?"

"The schoolteacher's in police custody, isn't he?"

"That's different."

"Why?"

"They want to kill him for himself. Killing me is incidental. I just happen to know something."

"What?"

"I have no idea. I stumbled over something in my pursuit of this English teacher. I don't know what I know, but they don't know that."

"Then you need protection."

"I haven't been abandoned. Cops are watching me."

"That will be small consolation when they watch you get shot."

"Alice, there's a cop outside right now. I call this number, tell him I'm going out, he meets me at the door. He gives me the all-clear, escorts me to my car, gets me on the road. Tags along to see I haven't got a tail."

Alice's eyes widened. "You're going to work?"

"We can't stop living—"

"You're going to *work*!"

"Alice—"

"Someone's trying to kill you, and you're going to work! You're going into these rough neighborhoods where you almost get killed anyway. These housing projects and drug dens where anyone can hide anywhere. You're going to make yourself a sitting duck, and it's all right, because some beat cop in a cruiser is going to see it happen!"

"You're getting all worked up."

"Are you crazy! These are mobsters! They shot one of their own because they weren't happy with his performance. They missed you, so you want to give them another chance?"

"You want me to hide from them forever while you walk Zelda and do the shopping and everything else?"

"Why not?"

"Because when I don't come out, they'll grab you."

Alice looked at me in horror. "Jesus Christ!"

"Yeah."

"You're serious."

"There are only two possibilities here. They're out to get me or they're not. If they're out to get me, they'll stop at nothing."

Alice looked pale. I took her by the arm. "There is a saving grace. The cops want these guys. They want 'em bad. They're gonna watch me very well."

"But why do you have to work?"

"I have to keep up appearances. If I seem to be going about my

222

business, the guys will either forget about me or make a move. Either way, it will wrap things up."

"But you don't have to *go* to work. You could *pretend* to work."

"What good would that do?"

"You could drive around to some nice neighborhoods. Safe buildings. Clean, new, well lit."

"The doorman will tell me to get lost."

"You can't talk your way past a doorman?"

"I have work for Richard."

"What work?"

"I have to be in court, for one thing. Testify in a case."

"Couldn't he put it off?"

"Alice."

"Let him get an adjournment. Or continuance. Or whatever the hell they call it. I mean, how important can it be?"

"The client's a quadriplegic."

"And if you put it off, Richard's afraid he might get *better*?" Alice said sarcastically.

My thoughts flashed to Richard's other client, Jerome Robinson, the man with the broken neck, miraculously improving every day. Could a quadriplegic get better? "Some things can't wait, Alice. I can't keep looking over my shoulder."

"Bad dialogue. You sound like a B-movie hero." Alice grabbed me, looked in my eyes. "Please. Be careful."

"I promise."

49

I DROVE OUT TO EAST NEW YORK. Not the type of place Alice would have approved of, but I had business. And I felt a little guilty about it, because I hadn't mentioned this business. I'd given Richard's court case as the reason I had to work, instead. Whereas actually I could have cared less about his damn quadriplegic, and I'm sorry if that's insensitive, but a short postponement wouldn't have killed anyone, because quadriplegics *don't* improve, and in the end it's just money.

The real reason I didn't want to stop working, the reason I hadn't given Alice, the reason I felt guilty about, was the mother with the dead baby I'd bullied Richard into helping. And it wasn't just that she was gorgeous, though she was. It was that I'd accomplished something, that I'd gotten some justice for somebody, and I'd done it by bending the rules, like some crazy TV detective who won't let the downtrodden suffer, who somehow finds a way. I'd done it, and I'd done it proud, and if the woman that I'd done it for happened to look like a supermodel, well, that was just too damn bad. It's not often in this business that I get to be the hero, and I wanted to play the scene.

I rang ahead to make sure she was home. Told her I had to see her. Didn't say why. She didn't argue. She was used to being told what to do by men. I said I was coming up, and that was that.

My cop buddy picked me up at my door. A burly young guy with a crew cut and no neck. A guy who, I realized, would have seemed like an older man not that long ago. He told me the street was clear and I could accompany him to my car. That was good, because I didn't know where my car was parked. The cops had towed it away and recovered the bullet and replaced the windshield. They hadn't bought me a new car seat. The fabric was merely patched, and cheaply at that, but I wasn't about to complain. I hopped in, pulled on the seat belt, happy to be alive.

"Where you headed?" the cop asked.

"East New York."

"Is that a good idea?"

"It's on the agenda."

He shrugged and hopped into his cruiser, which was double-parked right alongside. Handy being a cop. He backed up, and I pulled out.

I drove down Broadway to Ninety-sixth Street and got on the West Side Highway heading north. That must have confused him, since East New York is in Brooklyn. At the G.W. Bridge exit, I took the Cross-Bronx Expressway east, to I-87 south, to the Triboro Bridge. I took the Grand Central Parkway out past LaGuardia and Shea Stadium. At the exit for the Van Wyck, I bore right onto the Jackie Robinson Parkway. Under its old name, the Interboro Parkway, it would have given the cop a clue. The Interboro connects Brooklyn and Queens.

There was a method to my madness. My circuitous route had involved mainly highway driving, as opposed to picking my way though crowded city streets, where a sniper might be hiding.

I pulled up in front of Yolanda Smith's crack house. My cop wasn't keen on sending me in there, wanted to go along. I told him I was fine. It was an odd juxtaposition. In one of my scarier neighborhoods I actually felt safe.

Yolanda met me at the door. Showered, fresh, in a terry-cloth robe. Her hair was wet. She looked sensational.

"What is it?"

I smiled. "The lawyer's going to take your case."

"Yes!"

She clapped her hands, threw her arms around me, gave me a hug.

Did I do it just for that?

Absolutely not. Even if her bathrobe was slipping just a little.

I tried to keep it professional. After all, it was professional. Purely professional. I had no ulterior motive. Just to do the right thing. A white knight on a steed.

I sat her down, told her how it would be. She shouldn't get her hopes up. There might be problems. But the lawyer was willing to try.

She didn't understand. In her mind, if the lawyer was taking her case, that should be that. "I don't see what's so hard. I lost my baby. They were in the wrong."

"I told you. They'll lie. And we have no witnesses."

"What about Sean?"

"Who?"

"The director."

The porn director. "What about him?"

"Won't they believe him?"

I blinked. "I thought he was the one who told the doctor not to operate."

"That's right."

"So he's on the doctor's side."

"No, he's not. He out for hisself. Doctor did what he wants. Don't mean he'll do what the doctor wants. We could get some cash."

"We?"

"Enough for a video. Make me a star."

I blinked. "Wait a minute. You're saying the director will testify against the doctor, in return for which you'll split the settlement with him and he'll make a rap video with you?"

Her smile was enormous. "And everybody's happy."

Everybody except me.

What had I done? In my do-gooder, white-knight, Stanley-to-the-rescue mode, largely influenced by the fact that everything else had gone to hell, I had ignored Richard's better judgment, my own better judgment, and, had she known anything about it, Alice's better judgment, and committed myself to furthering the interests of a gold-digging wannabe porn star eager to feather her nest by winning a shaky medical malpractice case with the help of perjured testimony. Or, at least, paid testimony. And, while medical experts were paid for their time on the stand, porn directors weren't. When you paid for the testimony of a porn director, it wasn't something you could let the opposing counsel bring out in court, and say, so what, everybody does it. Everybody *didn't* do it, and if anybody found out you did it, your ass was grass.

My stomach felt hollow. Was it all for this that I had blackmailed my boss? Into a sleazy deal. Both for him and for me. A lose-lose situation. Him taking a case he didn't want. Me testifying to things that weren't true. Or, if not testifying to them, at least holding my tongue. Concealing evidence to bolster a client's case.

Well, wasn't that what lawyers do? Lawyers, yes. They present the facts they want and suppress the ones they don't. Argue that those presented by the opposition are meaningless. But I'm not a lawyer. I'm a private investigator. And that is not my job. My job is to tell what I know. Put on the stand, my job is to answer questions truthfully. Granted, I need answer no more than I'm asked. Even if I know what I will be asked. And what I won't be asked. And what not to touch on cross-examination. I can do that without feeling sleazy, can't I?

But this?

To have bartered that for this.

And to have come here, today, with police escort, at my own peril, in spite of threats of death and Alice's pleading.

I wanted to tell her to go to hell. I didn't even have the guts to do that. I just smiled and got the hell out of there.

My cop buddy was waiting right outside.

"Where to?" he said.

I had no idea.

50

ALICE WAS NO HELP. Odd for Alice. Alice usually has the answer for everything. I wondered if it had to do with the comeliness of the client. Which I hadn't particularly emphasized. Unless it had to do with the fact I *hadn't* particularly emphasized the comeliness of the client. Alice is rather astute in these matters. Of course, she might have got a hint from the fact the girl did skin flicks. A detail I was not quite able to leave out of the narrative. Even though I started with rap videos. Which in Alice's view is bad enough. Alice is not a huge fan of the rap video. Or the rap song, for that matter. She is not even willing to concede that it *is* a song. While I find this hard to dispute, just as I find all things hard to dispute with Alice, I am somewhat reluctant to agree, as it seems to push us even further down the slippery slope toward old fogeyhood.

Anyway, Alice had little or no sympathy for my plight. She couldn't believe I even cared.

"Stanley, they're shooting at you. And you're worried about a client."

"I'm not worried about the client."

"Then why did you bring it up?"

"You asked what's bothering me."

"So you *are* worried about it."

"Give me a break. Someone fired a shot at me. Meanwhile, life goes on. This happened today. After the shot. Perhaps not as important as the shot, but, hey, life goes on."

"Bra."

"Huh?"

"'Obladi, oblada, life goes on bra.' You know. The Beatles."

"I'm glad *I* didn't say that."

"Yeah. It's a Stanleyism."

"You're really scared, aren't you? Or you wouldn't be driving me nuts."

"That's not true."

"Right. You always drive me nuts. Look, suppose I take some time off."

"Because of this woman?"

"No! Because someone tried to shoot me."

"Oh, yeah? That happened, you couldn't care less. You went rushing right out there. Then this porn star pulls a number on you, you wanna climb back in your shell."

"She's not a porn star."

"So now you'd like to cut back on your cases?"

"Wouldn't you prefer if I did?"

"Yes, I'd prefer if you did. I'd prefer if you had today, before you went to see this girl, who's got you so confused you don't know what you're doing."

"I'll call Richard, I'll cut back on my cases."

"Don't cut back. Stop. Stay home. Let the cops sort this out. You got hitmen and mobsters involved, this is a little bit out of your league. No offense meant. But you're not going to solve this thing by walking around with a bull's-eye on your back."

"You mean stay in?"

"You're very bright! That's why I married you."

"I have to walk the dog," I protested.

"I'll walk the dog."

"I don't *want* you to walk the dog."

"Don't worry. I'll take the cop."

"He won't go."

"He will if you're not going anywhere. Just call him in and tell him."

I sighed. "Alice, I can't stay holed up forever."

"Not forever. Just until they catch this jerk." Alice went to the door. "Zelda's gotta go out. I'll get the cop, you tell him take me to the park."

"I don't like your going."

"Okay, I'll get the cop, you tell him to take *Zelda* to the park."

I shook my head. "This won't work."

"Maybe not, but it's what we're doing. At least for now. And tomorrow you call Richard and tell him you can't work. At all. You're not just cutting back. You're off the clock until further notice."

I grimaced. "Oh."

"What's the matter?"

"I can't do that."

"Why not?"

"I have to be in court."

51

I FELT LIKE CHARLES BRONSON in *The Valacchi Papers,* marching into court under armed guard to testify against the mob. After all, I had police protection. And there I was, going through the metal detectors up to Part 24. But here the resemblance endeth. I wasn't testifying against the mob, I was giving evidence in a negligence suit. No one would go to jail as a result of what I had to say. People would just lose money. Aside from that, it was pretty dramatic, and if I wanted to feel like Charlie Bronson, I certainly would.

It wasn't easy. For one thing, the courtroom wasn't jammed, the way it would have been in a Mafia hearing. The plaintiff wasn't even there. Richard had tried every trick in the book to get him into court, but the judge wasn't biting. A severe, needle-nosed lady in a black robe, who lacked only a black hat to pass for the Wicked Witch of the West, Judge Epstein was not easily swayed. For her money, a quadriplegic who could not breathe on his own, and who required elaborate medical apparatus just to keep him alive, did not have to be there. Still, I'd have laid you 8 to 5 on Richard's getting the sucker into that courtroom before the trial was over. In the meantime, he'd get a lot of mileage out of his client's absence.

Richard's loyal opposition consisted of three starchy-looking lawyers and one rather ratty-looking defendant whose age couldn't have been more than twenty-five and whose IQ might have been less. This unprepossessing young man was unlucky enough to own the building in which Richard's client had fallen, and would be on the hook for damages in the event that we won.

In the gallery, witnessing this historic battle, were three, count them, three spectators: a plump woman knitting a sweater, perhaps the defendant's mother; a young woman dressed as a prostitute, either the defendant's wife or a prostitute; and a drunk sleeping it off. Not the most menacing group imaginable; still, my bodyguard checked them out.

Richard hurried up to me. "Is this really necessary?" he said, indicating the cop.

"Speak to him."

"Could you give him a little room?"

"No."

Richard raised his eyebrows. "Excuse me?"

"I'm doing my job. You got a problem with that?"

"Not now, I don't. But when the jury's brought in, he looks like he's in custody."

"Just explain that he's not."

"Oh, sure," Richard scoffed. "If I try to tell them he's involved in a murder case, the judge won't let the jury hear it. If the judge *does* let the jury hear it, the defense will object and ask for a mistrial. They may not get it, but they'll get a continuance."

"What's wrong with that?"

"I got a kid on a ventilator needs money. These guys are going to pay it. The defense is using every trick in the book to stall. I'm not going to give 'em one on a silver platter."

"That's too bad."

"Yes, it is. So could you cut me a little slack?"

"What do you want?"

"Do you have to sit next to him?"

"I could sit behind him."

"That's almost as bad."

"Do you want it or not?"

Richard sighed. "Look, could you wait out in the hall?"

"Huh?"

"There's no reason for him to be in here anyway. Until you're called to the stand. Why don't you guys wait outside? Any objection to that?"

The cop shrugged. "Works for me."

"When he *is* called, think you could avoid marching him in?"

"I'm coming in when he does."

Richard wasn't happy with the answer. "He's going on the stand. Where are you going?"

"I'll sit in the closest available seat."

"Fine. Instead of escorting him down the aisle, do you think you could poke your head in the door like maybe you're one of the next witnesses to be called? Or maybe you just wanted to sit and read? I don't suppose you could carry a *New York Post*?"

"Give me a break."

"All right, but you get the picture. You think you can do that?"

The cop said, "Yeah, sure," but he muttered "Lawyers" under his breath as we headed up the aisle.

There was a bench right outside. We sat on it, my bodyguard next to me, defending me against the world, a small world consisting of a few cops, some extremely young prosecutors, and a few perpetrators, easily identified by their new suits, recent haircuts, and the handcuffs on their wrists.

I wished *I* had the *New York Post*. I could do the sudoku in it. Yeah, I'm hooked on 'em, too. Isn't everybody?

A few hours passed and nothing happened. Except once

Richard came out to tell us nothing happened. We probably could have figured that out for ourselves. Except when he said nothing, he *meant* nothing. The jury wasn't even in yet. He and the defense counsels were still arguing about procedure.

Richard went back in and nothing continued to happen for quite some time.

I was just nodding off when I was roused from my slumber by the patter of feet. Not little feet. Big-girl feet. As in heels that go clack, clack, clack. I hadn't been hearing many of those. Female ADAs, though well-dressed in skirts and pantsuits, opted for more practical footwear, knowing they'd be on their feet most of the day. I glanced up to see what newbie hadn't gotten the message.

My mouth fell open.

It was her. My favorite teacher. What's-her-name. Sheila Blaine. Miss Perky Breasts. Boy, was she a knockout in a pale green sheath with a low-cut top. Hair up on her head. Just as if she was going to the senior prom.

Her eyes widened when she saw me. I was sitting on the bench with a cop. I must have looked like I was under arrest.

"What are you doing here?" she asked.

"Just a witness. What are you doing here?"

She made a face. "I got jury duty."

"You're kidding. On this case?"

"What case?"

"This one. The one I'm testifying."

"You're *testifying*?" She sounded impressed.

"No big deal." My eyes twinkled. "There is no dress code, you know."

She looked puzzled, then smiled. "Oh. Yeah."

"What's with the outfit?"

"I don't want a criminal case. I thought if I looked like this, the defense attorney wouldn't want me."

"You're probably right. So, what case are you on?"

She shook her head. "I'm not on a case. I just got rejected."

"Then it wasn't this case. The jury's already selected."

"I don't know. It was a chain snatching. Is that you?"

"No. This is a civil suit. How come they didn't want you?"

"Too much education."

I said to the cop. "You mind if I talk to her alone? I think I can handle myself."

He gave me a look.

I ushered her to the next bench, sat her down.

"So he *is* with you."

"Yeah."

"Because of Marty?"

"Among other things."

"What other things?"

"The cops think I know something."

"Do you?"

"Not a damn thing."

"I don't understand."

"The cops think someone's out to get me just like they're out to get Kessler."

"Why?"

"Does Kessler know why?"

"No."

"There you are. It's a comedy of errors, a case of mistaken identity, just one colossal fuckup. But the bottom line is I got cops babysitting me."

"But . . ."

"But what?"

"You think they're after you just because you were involved with Marty?"

"And Victor Marsden."

"Exactly. So I don't understand . . ."

"What?"

"Why aren't they after me?"

52

WE HAD LUNCH AT A small diner near the courthouse. My cop wasn't happy about it, but I had to have lunch. Short of his going and getting it for me, which would have left me alone, I had to go out. If I wanted to eat with someone sightly more attractive than a NYPD flatfoot, that was my business. It was also none of his.

Sheila and I got a booth. The cop got a stool at the counter so he could watch the door. Not that he really expected someone to try to take me out in a crowded downtown diner during lunch. The odds for success did not equal the risk.

I ordered a cheeseburger and fries and a Diet Coke, wondered if she'd think me common. Wondered if I was an idiot for wondering that. I was way older than she was, I was happily married, and who gave a damn what she thought?

Men do.

Oh, how they do.

She had a club sandwich and an iced tea. I could have had an iced tea. I might have, if she'd ordered first. But when the waiter came, she was looking at the menu, and said, "Go ahead." And one doesn't stand on ceremony at a diner during lunch. They'd be zipping us in and out of this booth in thirty minutes, tops.

I said, "Is this your first day?"

"First day?"

"Of jury duty."

"Oh. Yes."

"Did they show you the movie?"

"Movie? What movie?"

"Why you should be proud to be a juror."

"Oh, is *that* what it was about?" Huge smile. "I nodded off."

"You didn't miss much. Who's teaching Kessler's classes?"

"They got a substitute."

"I wonder who'll pay for that. I know, the city, but what department? Education? Law enforcement?"

"It isn't funny."

Her nostrils were flaring. Her cheeks were red. Did I mention the top of the dress she was wearing? I'd have put her on a jury without asking a single question.

"I know it isn't. But it doesn't make much sense, either. Nothing makes much sense. Most cases you've got no clues. This case you've got nothing *but* clues. And they're all interconnected. And they all have something to do with you."

She looked at me in alarm.

Before she could say anything, the waiter put our drinks in front of us.

She took her iced tea, sipped it, said, "What do you mean?"

"Give me a break. You're Marsden's girlfriend."

"Ex-girlfriend."

"You're fooling around with Kessler. All right, you're not fooling around, you're just his friend. Marsden's supposed to hit Kessler. But he doesn't. He gets hit himself. For *not* hitting Kessler.

Then someone tries to take Kessler out and gets killed. I see you at a funeral, and suddenly people want to kill me." My eyes widened. "Could that be it?"

"What?"

"You. I talk to you, and I'm in danger."

"That's stupid."

"What could you have told me that would make me a risk?"

"Nothing. I don't know anything."

"Maybe you think you don't. But maybe Marsden let something slip. That's why he was whacked. Not for the other thing."

"But he didn't. How many times do I have to tell you. We broke up. I hadn't seen him in months."

At the counter, my cop was sipping coffee and looking grouchy. The bar stool couldn't have been comfortable. I thought about asking him to join us.

Yeah, right.

"When you gotta be back?" I asked her.

"Back?" She looked embarrassed and smiled. "I don't know. I was supposed to report back when they excused me. Then I ran into you. They must have sent us to lunch by now, but I don't know. You think I'm in trouble?"

"No problem. You got your ballot."

"Huh?"

"The paper they gave you when they excused you. You gotta turn it in when you go back, right? So they can call you again. But if you haven't turned it in, they can't call you."

"Is that right?"

"Think about it. They draw the ballots out of a drum. If yours isn't in there, they can't pick it. You hang on to that, you can never be called."

"Did you do that?"

I hadn't. When I served jury duty, I turned in my ballot like a good boy. But it had seemed like a hell of an idea.

Our food came. So did the cop's. I noticed he was having a cheeseburger, too. Somehow that did not cheer me. Quite the opposite.

Her club sandwich came with potato chips.

"Can I try your fries?" she said.

"Be my guest."

She ate a couple, and I felt a little less like the lowbrow slob dining with the princess.

"How come you didn't defer it?" I asked her.

"Oh, you can't anymore. It doesn't matter what you do. I hear even the lawyers and judges have to serve."

"I know. I meant postpone it. Until later."

"Oh. They wouldn't do it. I guess they needed people."

I frowned. That wasn't right. They always allowed deferments. An educated person like her shouldn't have let herself be talked into it. "Had you postponed before?"

"No. It's my first time. What a zoo, huh?"

"So, who's covering your classes?"

"Oh, they'll get a substitute. No big deal. Happens all the time."

"Jury duty?"

"No. Substitute teachers. Just call in, say you need a sub."

"You don't have to turn in a curriculum?"

"No. Substitutes just tread water until you're back. Mostly babysitting."

"A little hard on the kids."

"They love it. Less work."

"What if you get put on a long case?"

"I hope I don't."

"Everybody hopes they don't."

I chewed my cheeseburger.

She looked at her watch.

"What time is it?"

"Nearly twelve thirty. I gotta get back."

"Yeah, but you don't know when."

"I gotta go to the bathroom." She pushed her plate back, got up, and went out.

I liked that. No "powder my nose" or other euphemism. Just, I gotta go to the bathroom.

The window by my booth shattered. Shards of safety glass beaded into little balls. A bullet ricocheted off the Formica countertop with a pinging sound I will long remember.

Things happened fast. I didn't see most of them, because my cop launched himself into the air and landed on top of me, a bit of a surprise. I knew he was my bodyguard, but it wasn't like I was the president; his job wasn't to stand in front of the bullet. He seemed to think it was. He wrenched me from the booth, wrestled me to the ground.

From outside came the sound of gunfire, but no windows shattered. Just a few ricochets off concrete. And a dull thud.

I tried to look, but I had a few hundred pounds of cop on me.

I was not alone on the floor. Patrons had gotten down after the initial shock.

After the initial shot.

There was a cacophony of cries, shrieks, squeals, screams, wails, which all added up into an uneasy euphoria that no one was actually hit, that no one was actually hurt, that everyone was okay.

On top of me, the cop was fumbling with his walkie-talkie. "I have the target. Target is safe. Repeat, target is safe. Location secure."

I blinked.

It was a shock to realize that I was the target. I'd known it, but I hadn't known it. But when I heard it, I knew it was true.

I still couldn't get up. I raised my head, looked around.

The diner was a disaster area. Food strewn, as waiters and waitresses dove for cover.

As if from a time warp, as if from another movie, as if from a different reality than the one we were in, Sheila came back from the bathroom. She stepped around the corner, saw the carnage before her. The mass of humanity stirring on the floor.

She glanced around.

Her eyes met mine.

I'll never forget the look on her face. Raw, stark terror. It was just a momentary flash, but the image was forever seared into my brain, would haunt me for nights to come.

"Amanda Peet," I murmured.

And everything fell into place.

53

MACAULLIF WAS THE FIRST ONE through the door. That was a shock. I hadn't known he was there. "Is he hit?" he growled.

I could see why he might have asked. I was still flat out on the floor.

"I'm not hit," I sputtered. "I got a half a ton of cop on me. Get off, damn it."

"You can let him up," MacAullif said. "The shooter's down. The area's secure."

"Are you sure?" the cop said.

"I got a SWAT team out there says it is."

"You sure the shooter's down?"

"The shooter's dead. I'd have liked him alive, but that's Sergeant Thurman for you."

"Thurman's here?" I said, climbing out from under my nursemaid.

"Wouldn't have missed it. I mentioned he was on suspension, but it didn't register. He's probably gonna take some flak."

"Son of a bitch."

"We'd like you to ID the shooter. If you're not too shaken up."

"I'm fine. But I don't know him."

"Did you see him?"

"No."

"Then how do you know you don't?"

"If I'm right, I never saw him before."

"If you're right about what? I thought you didn't know what was going on."

"I didn't. Until now." I lowered my voice. "Don't let the girl get away."

"Who?"

"The schoolteacher. Miss Perky Tits. She fingered me."

"She *what*?"

"She set me up. Come on MacAullif, act your age."

"Give me a break. I got a crime scene outside looks like a war zone. I got news crews showing up. What am I gonna tell 'em?"

"Don't ask me. You won't tell 'em anything except hard facts, and I ain't got 'em."

"What *do* you have?"

"Idle speculation." I looked at my watch. "Damn. I gotta be back in court."

"Hey, shithead. I hate to be a pain, but what can I hold the girl on?"

I looked around. "Actually, I think she's gone."

"What!"

"Don't sweat it, she won't get far. She's a schoolteacher. You can talk to her after class."

"Damn it!" MacAullif hissed. "All right. You paid me back for turning you in. We're even. I give up. What's the score?"

"Off the record, I don't know the hitman, but I'll bet he worked for Tony Fusilli."

"Tony tried to hit you because of something Louie Russo told you?"

"No. Because of something I told Louie Russo."

"I thought you didn't tell him anything."

"I thought so too. Turns out I was wrong."

"So, what did you tell him?"

"My name."

54

"STATE YOUR NAME."

"Stanley Hastings."

"What is your occupation?"

That always throws me. I want to say actor or writer. In my mind, my private eye work is just a job-job, what I do between gigs. Only it's been a long time since the last gig.

"I'm a private investigator."

"Did you investigate a case involving Phillip Fairbourne?"

"Yes, I did."

"Did you meet Mr. Fairbourne personally?"

"Yes, I did."

"Where did you meet him?"

"Columbia-Presbyterian Hospital."

"Is that the first time you met my client?"

I hesitated.

"Can't you answer that?" Richard said.

"I can, but, technically, when I met him he wasn't your client. He didn't become your client until I signed him to a retainer."

"You signed him to a retainer?"

"Yes, I did."

"There in the hospital?"

"That's right."

"You took down the facts of the case?"

"Yes, I did."

"And did Mr. Fairbourne tell you how he was injured?"

The defense attorneys were caught between a rock and a hard place. If they objected to me relating what the client said, it would give Richard an excuse to bring him into court.

"He said he'd fallen in the building where he lives. He said he tripped on a broken stair."

"Did he tell you where that stair was?"

"Between the second and third floor. About three quarters of the way up."

"Did you see that stair yourself?"

"Yes, I did."

"How did you come to see that stair?"

"I did a Location of Accident photo assignment. I took pictures of the broken stair."

"When did you do that with relation to when you interviewed Mr. Fairbourne in the hospital?"

"I did it the same day."

"Do you have those photos here in court?"

"Yes, I do."

"Could you produce them, please."

Richard then went through the painstaking process of marking the photos for identification. When we were done, Richard asked that they be introduced into evidence.

The defense attorney was on his feet. "I'd like to ask a few questions on voir dire."

"Proceed," the judge said.

The defense attorney approached me as if I were the ebola virus. "You took these pictures?"

"Yes, I did."

"You say that was on the same day you signed the client to a retainer?"

"Yes, it was."

"You did this in conjunction with your job?"

"That's right."

"By whom are you employed, Mr. Hastings?"

"Actually, I'm self-employed."

He smiled as smugly as if I'd just confessed to stealing the Kleinschmidt diamonds. "Well, that's a nice evasion, Mr. Hastings."

"Objection, Your Honor," Richard said. "Would you please instruct counsel that he is supposed to ask questions, not characterize true answers as evasions."

The defense attorney feigned surprise. "Your Honor, whether or not the witness is evading the question is entirely relevant."

"And you're free to demonstrate it. You're not allowed to simply state it. Not on voir dire."

"You want me to *ask* him if he's evading the question?"

"You're free to do so."

"Mr. Hastings, are you evading the question?"

"I'm just trying to be accurate. I'm an independent contractor, a self-employed sole proprietor of my business. I take individual cases and subcontract my services to various law firms."

"Including that of Richard Rosenberg, the attorney for the plaintiff in this lawsuit?"

"That's right."

"Were you working for Mr. Rosenberg when you took these pictures?" The attorney's smile was smug. "If you'd like to evade the question, feel free."

Richard sprang to his feet. "Oh, Your Honor."

Judge Epstein banged her gavel. "That will do. Jurors will disregard the last remark. Witness will answer the question."

"My agency was employed by Mr. Rosenberg."

"When you saw the plaintiff in the hospital, you signed him to a retainer?"

"That's right."

"What was the attorney's name on the retainer?"

"Richard Rosenberg."

"Well, forgive me for assuming you were evading the question," the attorney said sarcastically. "So, these photos you allegedly took, which Mr. Rosenberg is offering into evidence—"

"Object to the word *allegedly,* Your Honor."

"Overruled. The witness can clarify in his answer."

"When you *allegedly* took those photos, who were you working for then?"

"I was *allegedly* working for Richard Rosenberg."

The defense attorney scowled.

The judge had a narrow escape from a grin.

"How much money were you paid for these photos?"

"I can't say, exactly. I assume it was a two- or three-hour assignment."

"A hundred dollars?"

"It's possible."

"More?"

"It's possible."

"As much as a thousand."

"Absolutely not."

"How do you know?"

"If I'd made a thousand bucks, believe me, I'd know."

"Are you being paid for your time in court?"

"Yes, I am."

"Who is paying you?"

"Richard Rosenberg of Rosenberg and Stone."

"He pays your salary?"

"I explained it's not a salary."

"He pays your fees?"

"That's right."

"Oh, Your Honor," Richard objected. "This is voir dire."

"Yes, it is," the defense attorney said. "The witness has identi-fied these photographs. He has testified when he took them. The last is very much in question. The bias of the witness is entirely relevant."

"I will stipulate this is a friendly witness," Richard said.

"That's not enough, Your Honor. If the witness is biased in the plaintiff's favor, if he has a monetary stake in the outcome of the case, that's something I have every right to bring out."

"Proceed," Judge Epstein ruled.

"Are you biased in the plaintiff's favor?"

"I barely know the plaintiff."

"You are employed by the plaintiff's side of the case. Including his attorney, Mr. Rosenberg. Are you telling me you're not biased in their favor?"

"Oh, absolutely."

"You're absolutely not biased in their favor?"

"No, I absolutely am."

"What?"

"I'm biased in their favor. I want them to win."

Judge Epstein squinted down from the bench. "Excuse me, Mr. Hastings. Are you aware of what you're saying? Of what the words mean? Just because you're working for someone, doesn't mean you're biased for them. Bias indicates a prejudice that colors your testimony regardless of the truth. Is that what you claim?"

"I mean to tell the truth, Your Honor. But if I can slant it the plaintiff's way, I'm certainly going to. I'm also going to do every-thing in my power to hurt the defense."

Judge Epstein blinked. "Excuse me? What did you just say?"

"Besides being biased for the plaintiff, I'm also biased against the defense."

The attorney looked like he'd just won the lottery. "Wait a minute. Let me be sure the jury understood that. You say you are biased against the defendant in this case?"

"That's right."

"Do you know the defendant?"

"No, I do not."

The attorney was practically rubbing his hands together. "Then why are you biased against him?"

"He tried to have me shot."

55

I HUNTED UP MACAULLIF IN his office. He looked none the worse for wear. "You on paid leave too?" I asked him.

"I should be so lucky. If I'd killed the fucker, I would be. Unfortunately, Thurman did, so I get dick."

"What was Thurman doing there?"

"Following you. He's been tailing you ever since they shot up your car."

"Why?"

"Because he's not as smart as you."

"Huh?"

"He's not smart enough to overthink everything with tortuous logic. Thurman goes straight for the obvious. If someone is shooting at you, it must be because they want you shot. Granted, that's probably not enough for you to wrap your mind around, but that's all it was."

"What were you doing there?"

"Thurman called me."

"You're kidding."

"Said you were out to lunch with a piece of ass."

"That's news?"

"You seen yourself lately? No way a girl like that gives you a tumble."

"Thanks a lot."

"Hey, even Thurman thought it stank. You, of course, *expect* Angelina Jolie to fall for you. But in the *real* world, you don't rate a second look. Thurman called me, and I came by to see for myself."

"Why?"

"It's only two blocks. I needed a good laugh."

"No, really."

"I asked Thurman to give me a call if you did anything dumb. I expected the phone to ring off the hook. Actually, he didn't call till you picked up a girl."

"I didn't pick up a girl."

"No, she picked you up. Which should have been your first clue. A hot babe like that picking up an old fart like you."

It should have. But I'd blown it. And so had Alice, actually, if I wanted to bring it up. Not that I ever would. But with all the politically correct *he*ing and *she*ing and *him*ing and *her*ing, the whole time we'd been talking about a hitman when we should have been talking about a hitperson. To allow for the possibility of a hitwoman. Which, in fact, there was.

Hitman #3 was Hitperson #3.

Hitwoman #3.

Amanda Peet.

And once you accepted that, it all made sense.

Sort of.

"Run it by me again," MacAullif said.

"Aw, hell."

I'd already made a statement for Crowley, with a lawyer and stenographer and the whole bit. Richard was there to get me immunity, which he did. Of course, the same didn't hold true for MacAullif, if Crowley wanted to make a stink. So he had more than an academic interest.

"You can read my statement," I told him.

"Yeah, but they may question me before I get a chance to read your statement. I'd like to be on the same page."

Sergeant Thurman came in. Which was a little odd. You can't kiss off someone who saved your life. Jesus Christ, was I now his genie, bound to serve his every whim?

Thank god, he didn't throw his arms around me, make a fuss, or even ask how I was. From Thurman's point of view, he'd done his job, and that was that.

Except it *wasn't* his job, he was on leave on account of the other shooting, and by rights he shouldn't have been there at all.

"Are you in trouble?" I asked.

He shrugged. "Nah. They're so happy to get these guys, I get a free ride."

"Do you know what happened?" MacAullif asked. He shouldn't have. A Sergeant Thurman explanation is an oxymoron.

Thurman wasn't even going to try. "Don't know, don't care. The bad guys went down, it'll all get sorted out."

Thurman flopped into a chair as if he were there to watch baseball. He'd have looked natural with a Lite Beer.

"Stanley was just about to tell us," MacAullif said. "Go on, Stanley."

It was a little weird with Thurman there. But there was that whole genie thing. "Okay, I'd been thinking about the case upside down. The minute I realized I was the target, things fell into place."

"Hey," MacAullif said. "We're not interested in a self-congratulatory diatribe on your powers of deduction."

"Damn, you speak well for a cop," I said. If MacAullif was going to mock me in front of Thurman, I wasn't just going to take it.

"Asshole. I'm on the hook here. For trying to help you out. You wanna stop whacking off long enough to give me a reach-around?"

Thurman chuckled at that.

"That sounds more like a cop."

"Come on, asshole."

"Okay. Victor Marsden is a hitman for the mob. For years he's carried out hits on low-level thugs and hoods, as befits a mob hitman."

"Listen to this guy," MacAullif told Thurman. "He says *befits,* and he makes fun of how *I* talk."

"What happens? Marsden is asked to kill someone else. Someone with no connections to the mob whatsoever. A family man with a wife and kid who wouldn't hurt a fly. I assumed it was Martin Kessler, just like everyone else. I was shocked to find out it was me."

"Why'd they want to kill you?" Thurman asked.

I could see MacAullif loading up a wisecrack. I hurried along. "Because I handled the case of Phillip Fairbourne, the quadriplegic who fell in a stairway in East Harlem. The building is managed by J.T.C. Realty."

"Which is run by the mob?" Thurman said.

"No. Which is run by Chester T. Markowitz, the nicest Jewish gentleman one would ever want to meet."

"They let Jews in the mob?" Thurman said.

I refrained from rolling my eyes. It was hard to hate a guy who saved your life. If it could have been anyone else. "No. But J.T.C. Realty is insured by Prime Metro, an independent insurance company offering catastrophic coverage at exorbitant rates."

"Why would anyone buy from them?"

"They got a talking lizard and they advertise on TV."

Thurman's eyes widened. "They're Geico?"

MacAullif shot me a warning look.

"No. They're Tony Fusilli's idiot nephew. They bust heads.

255

They come in, they say, 'Do you want to switch to our coverage, yes you do.' Most people switch. Otherwise, they have business problems. Like their store burns down.

"Tony Fusilli's idiot nephew tried to sell J.T.C. Realty an insurance policy. They balked at the amount. Bad move. The young psychopath, deeply offended, made a counteroffer: J.T.C. Realty would take the insurance and sell him one of its properties at a criminally negligible price.

"So the idiot nephew winds up owning a building. He immediately sells himself insurance, and pays himself a commission on the sale. Which is all well and good until Prime Metro, a wholly owned subsidiary of Tony Fusilli Enterprises, is suddenly on the hook for umpty million dollars because a quadriplegic fell in the building and he's gonna sue."

I pressed on, before Sergeant Thurman could ask how a quadriplegic could fall in a building. "I handled the case. Took the Location of Accident pictures of the broken stairs. Which were in bad repair. Pretty clear-cut case. Slam dunk. Except no one wants to pay that kind of money, so they immediately begin covering up. The stairs are repaired overnight. The super is set to swear they were repaired before the accident. Only I got the pictures, and I can testify to when they were taken. The jurors take one look at the quadriplegic, and the steps that caused the accident, and the fact they tried to cover it up, and Tony Fusilli and his idiot nephew will be on the hook.

"So I gotta go.

"Victor Marsden is chosen for the task.

"To the man's credit, he didn't want to do it. He checked me out, couldn't justify taking my life. So he came up with a unique solution. He asked me if I'd help him try not to. Of course, he couldn't tell me I was the mark, that would have defeated his own purpose. So he refused to tell me who it was. Said if I found out on my own, it was my business.

"He also wouldn't give me his name. He knew I'd check him out, and I'd never work for Victor Marsden. So he tells me he's Martin Kessler. For two reasons. One practical, one whimsical. Kessler has no record, will check out clean. And, Kessler is involved with his ex-girlfriend. If I make trouble for Martin Kessler, that's the icing on the cake.

"While I'm checking Kessler out, the boys lean on Marsden pretty hard. How come I'm still alive? Is he slipping? What's the problem?

"Marsden assured them everything is fine, but no one is taking his word for it. So they put Frankie Delgado on him."

"Hitman Number 2?" MacAullif said.

It took me back to hear someone voicing that appellation besides Alice. I forgot I'd told MacAullif. "Right," I said. "And what does he see? He sees Marsden arrange a chance meeting with me in a bar. At least, that's how it looks to him. Hitman Number 2, I mean. Marsden has told me he's gonna pretend it's a chance meeting. So I play right along. So, Hitman Number 2 sees Marsden scope me out, double-check the ID.

"What's next is Phony Double-Dealing, Double-Tailing one-oh-one. I am 'hired' to tail Marsden to see if anyone is taking an interest in him. I am told not to pick him up at the school where he teaches because he doesn't want me seen there. The reason he doesn't want me *seen* there, is because he doesn't *work* there. I will, instead, pick him up outside of *my* building. Without acknowledging his presence or making any move on him. In case someone should be watching.

"Someone *is* watching. That's the whole point.

"So I tail Marsden. But, as far as the person watching is concerned, because we are making no contact, and constantly shifting positions in a gigantic do-si-do, it looks like Marsden picked me up at my office and is tailing me.

"What happens? I lead Marsden a merry chase and go back to my office. At which point he hangs it up and goes home.

"I follow.

"Marsden, savvy guy that he is, realizes he's got two tails. He hangs out in the lobby, receives Hitman Number 2, ushers him up to his apartment. Goes out and convinces yours truly that Hitman Number 2 lives there and Hitman Number 2 is the mark. He sends me on my way, and goes back home and convinces Hitman Number 2 that there is no problem and I will be out of their hair tomorrow.

"Not good enough. Tony Fusilli is pissed to find out I am still alive, and orders Marsden hit."

"So why were they shooting Martin Kessler?" Thurman asked.

"They were never shooting Martin Kessler. They were always shooting me. They tried to shoot me through the window of Martin Kessler's apartment. And they made a pass at me in front of the high school. Hitman Number 2 shows up, and Sergeant Thurman shoots him dead."

"I know I should have read him his rights," Thurman said. "But it takes too long. The guy would have reloaded."

Oh, my god. Thurman made a joke. Hell must have frozen over.

"So they bring in Hitman Number 3. Amanda Peet."

"Huh?"

"Hitwoman Number 3. Sheila Blaine. Who is on the scene already. She's Marsden's ex-girlfriend, and she's still in the mob. She's already met me and knows what I look like. The perfect person to set me up."

"How'd you figure out they were after you?"

"I didn't. But I should have. The real clue was Louie Russo. I talked to him in the lobby of Tony Fusilli's building. The next thing I know he winds up dead. The obvious answer is Louie let something slip. Only he didn't. The other solution is I let something slip that let them know I'm a threat. Only I didn't do that either.

"Or so it would appear.

"In point of fact, I actually told Louie something."

"What?" Thurman asked.

"My name. He asked me for identification. I showed him my license. Stanley Hastings, private eye. That's what I told Louie, and that's what Louie told Tony Fusilli. And that's what made Tony mad enough to beat him to death with whatever was handy.

"Tony's been trying to have me killed for a week. Here I walk into his building, tell Louie I want to see Tony, and Louie sends me packing. Tony can't believe it. The dumb schmuck actually sent me away.

"So, with the court date approaching and time running out, we have a daring daylight move. They take a shot at me the next morning when I get in my car. It misses, and the arrival of a traffic cop foils any second attempt.

"The police take it seriously enough to assign me a cop. He's no secret service agent but good enough to keep the wolf at bay." I grimaced. "Did I really say 'wolf at bay'? I think you can get kicked out of the Private Eye Writers of America for that."

"Schmuck," MacAullif said.

"The unthinkable happens. I make it to court. They gotta figure some way to get me out. Fusilli's lawyers stall like crazy to keep me off the stand."

"Fusilli's lawyers?"

"The idiot nephew hired them, but we know who's footing the bill. Anyway, that's what's happening in court. But it won't last forever. They gotta get me out of there.

"So, they bring in Hitman Number 3. Marsden's ex. I met her before, so it's natural for her to talk to me. They send her to the courthouse to pick me up. Her cover story is she's doing jury duty. But she isn't prepped, and she makes mistakes. She didn't know what a ballot was. And she thought there were no more deferments instead of no more exemptions."

"Gee. If she was less attractive, that might have tipped you off," MacAullif said.

I ignored the comment. "Her job is simple. Take me out to lunch and sit me in the window. For Hitman Number 4."

"Who missed." MacAullif cocked his head at Thurman. "If you hadn't shot him, he'd have been in deep shit."

"I don't understand about the girl," Thurman said. "How'd she get involved? I thought she was a schoolteacher."

"She was. But she met Marsden. Went with him for two years. She claimed she never knew what he did. That's bullshit. She not only knew about it, she helped him do it. When they split up, she still had mob connections. Which had to be embarrassing for him. That's probably why he tweaked her by using her current boyfriend's name."

"Can you prove all that?" MacAullif said.

I shook my head. "None of it. But, hey, it's not my case. Crowley's the one who has to prove it. Which won't be easy with the hitman dead."

"Sorry about that," Thurman said. "But guess what? The dumb fuck had caller ID. Crowley's tracing his phone calls now. By the time he gets done, everyone is going down."

"Including the girl?"

MacAullif gave me his best I-am-dealing-with-a-moron look. "The one who tried to have you killed?" He cocked his head. "I think you could safely say Harmon High is going to be needing a substitute teacher."

58

I CAUGHT UP WITH RICHARD before he left the office. He was not in a good mood. "Well, they got a continuance," he groused. "Which is hardly fair. They get what they wanted for trying to kill my witness."

"How long?"

"Six weeks."

I groaned. "I gotta spend the next six weeks looking over my shoulder to see if Fusilli hired anyone else?"

"No. We're taking your deposition tomorrow. After that, even if they kill you, we can read it into the record."

"Somehow I find that small consolation."

"Don't be a dope. If it will do him no good to kill you, he won't bother."

"I understand the concept. This is a guy who murdered his own henchman in a blind fury for not mentioning my name."

"Once again, money was involved."

"Speaking of which?"

"What?"

"The Yolanda Smith case."

"I told you I'll take it."

"Drop it."

"Huh?"

"It's a bad case. You don't want it."

"I *know* it's a bad case. *You* made me take it."

"I shouldn't have done that. Drop the case."

Richard peered at me narrowly. "You're getting cold feet? You don't want to testify in the Jerome Robinson case?"

"I don't give a damn about the Jerome Robinson case. You're suing the City of New York. I don't think they'll send a hitman to stop me."

"That's not what I meant."

"I know what you meant. I took the pictures, you can do anything you want with them. You put me on the stand, I'll identify them. You can ask me anything. You know what questions to ask. But I'm not gonna lie. If they ask me if there are any *other* pictures, I'll tell them. But they're not gonna think to ask me, are they?"

"No." Richard frowned. "You really want me to drop the Yolanda Smith case?"

"Yeah."

"How come?"

"It's gonna be bolstered by the perjured testimony of a pornographer with a financial interest in the outcome."

Richard shrugged. "What's the down side?"

There endeth the story of the hitman with the heart of gold. Poor son of a bitch. If he'd just whacked me, as ordered, none of this would have happened. But, no, the schmuck had to have a conscience. Considered me too good to kill. I resent that. I'm worth killing as much as the next guy.

I don't know how Marsden's scenario played out. In his head, I mean. Would he make an unsuccessful pass at me that alerted the cops, that resulted more or less in what eventually happened? Or would he finally say "Aw, fuck it" and whack me? Having afforded me two or three extra days of life for being a nice guy. Whatever his intention, he didn't deserve to die. At least not for that. I'm sure he deserved to die ten times over for his various transgressions. But it's sort of nice to think that, no matter how bad he had been, he managed to do one decent thing in his life.

Of course, it killed him.

I turned in my time sheets, got in my car, and drove home.

No one tried to shoot me.